Dear Reader,

We're thrilled that some of Harlequin's most famous families are making an encore appearance! With this special Famous Families fifty-book collection, we are proud to offer you the chance to relive the drama, the glamour, the suspense and the romance of four of Harlequin's most beloved families— the Fortunes, the Bravos, the McCabes and the Cavanaughs.

You'll begin your journey at the Double Crown ranch in Red Rock, Texas, home of the legendary Fortunes and the setting of the twelve-book miniseries Fortunes of Texas: Reunion. Members of the family are preparing to honor their patriarch, Ryan Fortune, but a bloodred moon offers a portent of trouble ahead. As the clan deals with a mysterious body, an abduction, a health crisis and numerous family secrets, each member also manages to find love and a happily-ever-after you'll want to share.

We hope you enjoy your time in Red Rock. Be prepared for our next stop, the Rising Sun Ranch in Medicine Creek, Wyoming, where *USA TODAY* bestselling author Christine Rimmer kicks off the story of the Bravo family. Watch for *The Nine-Month Marriage,* the first of the Bravo series, beginning in March!

Happy reading,

The Editors

MAUREEN CHILD

is a California native who loves to travel. Every chance they get, she and her husband are taking off on another research trip. The author of more than sixty books, Maureen loves a happy ending and still swears that she has the best job in the world. She lives in Southern California with her husband, two children and a golden retriever with delusions of grandeur. Visit Maureen's website, www.maureenchild.com.

FAMOUS FAMILIES

the FORTUNES

USA TODAY bestselling author

MAUREEN CHILD

Fortune's Legacy

TORONTO NEW YORK LONDON
AMSTERDAM PARIS SYDNEY HAMBURG
STOCKHOLM ATHENS TOKYO MILAN MADRID
PRAGUE WARSAW BUDAPEST AUCKLAND

Special thanks and acknowledgment are given to Maureen Child for her contribution to the Fortunes of Texas: Reunion series.

To the readers of category romance. You are the reason we write. The reason we dream. Thank you all.

Recycling programs
for this product may
not exist in your area.

ISBN-13: 978-0-373-36490-9

FORTUNE'S LEGACY

Copyright © 2005 by Harlequin Books S.A.

This edition published by arrangement with Harlequin Books S.A.

For questions and comments about the quality of this book please contact us at Customer_eCare@Harlequin.ca.

www.Harlequin.com

Printed in U.S.A.

FAMOUS FAMILIES

The Fortunes

Cowboy at Midnight by Ann Major
A Baby Changes Everything by Marie Ferrarella
In the Arms of the Law by Peggy Moreland
Lone Star Rancher by Laurie Paige
The Good Doctor by Karen Rose Smith
The Debutante by Elizabeth Bevarly
Keeping Her Safe by Myrna Mackenzie
The Law of Attraction by Kristi Gold
Once a Rebel by Sheri WhiteFeather
Military Man by Marie Ferrarella
Fortune's Legacy by Maureen Child
The Reckoning by Christie Ridgway

The Bravos by Christine Rimmer

The Nine-Month Marriage
Marriage by Necessity
Practically Married
Married by Accident
The Millionaire She Married
The M.D. She Had to Marry
The Marriage Agreement
The Bravo Billionaire
The Marriage Conspiracy
His Executive Sweetheart
Mercury Rising
Scrooge and the Single Girl

The McCabes by Cathy Gillen Thacker

Dr. Cowboy
Wildcat Cowboy
A Cowboy's Woman
A Cowboy Kind of Daddy
A Night Worth Remembering
The Seven-Year Proposal
The Dad Next Door
The Last Virgin in Texas
Texas Vows: A McCabe Family Saga
The Ultimate Texas Bachelor
Santa's Texas Lullaby
A Texas Wedding Vow
Blame It on Texas
A Laramie, Texas Christmas
From Texas, With Love

The Cavanaughs by Marie Ferrarella

Racing Against Time
Crime and Passion
Internal Affair
Dangerous Games
The Strong Silent Type
Cavanaugh's Woman
In Broad Daylight
Alone in the Dark
Dangerous Disguise
The Woman Who Wasn't There
Cavanaugh Watch
Cavanaugh Heat

Chapter 1

"Henry Stevens got that promotion, damn it." Kyra Fortune wanted to kick something. Hard. But she wasn't willing to damage a brand-new pair of designer heels, so she squelched the urge.

"I heard," her assistant said glumly.

Kyra turned around to face the other woman in her office. Tracy Hudson's pixielike features were drawn into a blend of sympathy and disappointment.

"What exactly did you hear?" Kyra asked, knowing full well that the grapevine in Voltage Energy Company was bound to have complete details by now. And all *she* really knew was that she'd been passed over for promotion.

Again.

True, in the years she'd been at Voltage, she'd steadily climbed the corporate ladder to associate VP in the expansion division. But it wasn't fast enough for her. Her own annual review was still months away and she knew that if promotions were being made now, by the time it was her turn, there wouldn't be a slot left to give to her. No matter what she did to earn it.

Tracy set her memo pad down on her lap, leaned forward and got into some serious dirt dishing. "Mr. Stevens's assistant, Jolie, told Pam in accounting, who told Jacob in the mail room who just told me ten minutes ago.…"

In spite of the fury still tickling her insides, Kyra was forced to admire the flow of information. If the top dogs in this company thought they could keep a secret, they really ought to step out of their ivory towers once in a while. "Told you what?"

"You're not going to like it."

"Goes without saying," Kyra pointed out and, reaching down, snatched up a silver-plated letter opener. Bouncing the blade end of the thing against her palm, she waited.

"Apparently Mr. Wolff told Mr. Stevens that his work was 'exemplary' and—"

"Exemplary?" Kyra repeated, stunned to her toes.

"The man can't find the executive bathroom without a guide."

Tracy's lips twitched, then flattened out again. "He also said that Mr. Stevens had a promising future here and—"

"God," Kyra muttered, tossing the letter opener onto her desk. "There's more?"

"Mr. Wolff gave him the corner office on twenty-six."

An unpleasant little squeaky noise escaped Kyra's throat. "Twenty-six? The office with the blue walls and the built-in bookcases?"

"The very one."

Yes. The very one Kyra had been mentally redecorating for the last month. Ever since Myrna Edgington had given up that office to stay at home with her kids. Kyra couldn't quite understand the former executive's motivation, but she herself had been hoping to take over Myrna's old office. It was so Kyra. It was perfect. And damn it, she'd earned it.

She'd been so positive that no one would be able to deny the good work she'd been doing for the company.

Yet it appeared that while she waited months for her shot at another notch up the ladder of success, other people were stepping on her head on the way to the top. Didn't seem to matter how hard she worked, how many clients she brought into the fold at Voltage. All that counted around here was if Garrett Wolff approved of you or not.

And apparently, Kyra thought with a disgusted sigh, he didn't approve of her.

Not exactly a news flash.

Her immediate supervisor was a tall, gorgeous hunk of mean. Garrett never took her seriously. He always looked at her as if he half expected her to show up in tennis whites and serve a backhand across the boardroom table. All because her last name was Fortune.

She glanced around her office, taking in the softly soothing pale-lavender walls, the carefully chosen art sprinkled around the room, and the comfortable, yet businesslike chairs. She'd made a place for herself here. Put her own personal stamp on what would have been a distinctly impersonal junior executive's office.

But she wanted more.

She couldn't help it. That was just who she was. She knew darn well that some people considered her spoiled. But Kyra didn't think of herself like that. She wasn't spoiled. She was…appreciated.

And why shouldn't she be? she argued silently. She worked hard. She didn't trade on her family name. She came in early and went home late. She could have gone to work for Fortune TX, Ltd. when she left college. But she hadn't. Hadn't wanted anyone to be able to stand back and accuse her of being successful simply because she was a Fortune.

She'd come to Voltage specifically to avoid any whispers of nepotism. And it had worked. In fact, she'd had to work even harder here to prove herself than anyone else. As far as she could see, at Voltage, her family name almost worked against her. Damn it, she'd earned every step she'd taken up the corporate ladder, and she wouldn't stop until she reached the top.

No matter how hard her arch nemesis, Garrett Wolff, tried to prevent her from succeeding.

Just thinking about the man could make Kyra grind her teeth in frustration. Every time she was around him, her skin hummed and her temper flared. He was a match to her stick of dynamite.

To hide her feelings, she turned away from Tracy's too-knowing gaze and stared out the window.

The spring sky was the kind of blue you only found in Red Rock, Texas—as bright and sharp a color as the bluebonnets that dotted every meadow in the state. A few high, white clouds scudded across the wide expanse of sky and tossed shadows onto the buildings below. Just outside San Antonio, but officially within the city limits, Kyra thought wryly, the business park had all the charm of a maximum security prison.

The buildings were tall and bland. The landscaping consisted of tiny patches of grass with the occasional baby tree, boasting a branch and a half each, plopped down in the center of said patch. No flowers brightened the sterile environment. Actually, there was no color at all, except for the postage stamp-size splotches of green. The windows in the buildings were mirrored, so that a view only gained you a picture of another building from a different angle.

It would have helped if she'd been able to open up one of her windows and actually *feel* some real Texas air sweeping in. But they were all sealed tightly, with the gentle hum of an air conditioner blowing recycled air through the rooms, mimicking the wind.

And she wouldn't even mind the ugly view or the sameness that hung over the ugly business park—if her view had been from the corner office on twenty-six.

This was all Garrett Wolff's fault.

In her mind's eye, she saw him, as she did every morning. Mr. Tall, Blond and Oblivious. He looked like a Nordic god and had all the charm of one as well. He rarely looked at Kyra, and when he did, she sensed his disapproval.

Well, too bad.

If he thought for one minute that she was going to be swayed by this last, completely illogical decision of his, he had another think coming. Kyra Fortune never gave up. Never quit.

"There's still one more promotion to be filled," Tracy stated, in a determinedly cheerful tone.

"True," Kyra agreed with a sigh. "But I'm not up for review again until October." She turned around, pulled out her high-backed, leather desk chair and plopped down onto it. Leaning back, she thought of all the things she'd like to say to Garrett Wolff.

She'd like to stomp down to the elevator, ride it to the top, charge past his übereffficient and mildly terrifying administrative assistant, Carol Summerhill, then personally flatten him with a few pithy, well-chosen insults.

But she wouldn't.

Because to advance at Voltage, she needed to impress, not threaten, Garrett Wolff.

Damn it.

"Kyra?"

She ran the tips of her manicured nails across that letter opener in an idle, stroking motion.

Tracy snapped her fingers a few times.

Jolted out of her thoughts, Kyra smiled at her friend. "Sorry. Daydreaming."

Tracy's dark brown eyes sparkled with humor. "And in this daydream, did you get away with arranging an 'accident' for Mr. Wolff?"

This is why she worked so well with Tracy. Sarcasm came in handy and a sense of humor was essential. "Not only got away with it," she said, leaning forward and grinning with real relish, "I took over his job and personally held the very tasteful memorial in his honor."

"Ooh," Tracy said, smiling. "Nice touch."

"I thought so." Kyra straightened up in her chair, checked her desk calendar with a quick glance, then shifted her gaze to Tracy. "Anyway, promotions, daydreams and wayward wishes aside, we still need to get some business done."

"Right." Tracy flipped open her memo pad, clicked her pen and got ready.

"Okay, then." Kyra pulled a file folder off the stack at her right and said, "Let's get started with the Hartsfield letter. We need to get the property rights tied up before Fortune TX, Ltd. steps in and claims them."

"You're always one step ahead, Boss," Tracy said, nodding in approval.

"It's the only way," Kyra agreed, and tried to push thoughts of Garrett Wolff to the back of her brain.

At least for the moment.

Garrett couldn't push thoughts of Kyra aside today. Not when his superiors were making such a pitch for him to promote the damn woman.

As senior VP of the expansion division, he should

be able to make these calls himself. But he knew better than most just how slippery the slopes were in corporate America.

He'd been at Voltage since leaving college, and he'd eventually worked himself into a position of power. And yet he was being coerced into promoting a woman he didn't feel was ready for the job.

All because of her name.

Disgusted, Garrett stood up, walked across the plush, dark blue carpet toward a credenza on the far wall. Inside the gleaming wood cabinet sat a coffeemaker. He reached for a heavy porcelain mug and poured himself a cup. Carrying the steaming brew with him, he stalked back to his desk and reread the memo that had arrived only an hour before.

Wolff—
See to a review of Kyra Fortune, then arrange her promotion. As discussed, make no mention of her family ties, but assure Ms. Fortune that her talents are appreciated and valued. Make this happen.
Henderson

Miles Henderson. CEO of Voltage Energy Company. A man with a mission. Garrett suspected Miles was determined to push through a merger with Fortune TX, Ltd. and he wanted Kyra to give him leverage. The board had decided in an emergency meeting the night before that Kyra, by virtue of being a Fortune, would be just the edge they needed when dealing with Fortune TX, Ltd.

Garrett set his coffee cup down on his uncluttered, ebony desktop and then leaned back in his chair. Damned if a part of him didn't almost feel sorry for the woman. She'd never traded on her name. Never made an issue of it at all.

If she got wind of the truth behind this promotion… Hell, he wasn't sure what she'd do.

His intercom buzzed. "Yes?"

"Ms. Fortune is here, sir."

"Fine, Carol. Send her in."

He stood up behind his desk, buttoned his suit jacket and prepared to lie his ass off.

She stepped into the room, then closed the door behind her. Walking across his office, she moved with an innate sense of grace, hips swaying, a cautious smile on her face. She was tall—about five foot nine—with a slender build and platinum-blond hair a few shades lighter than his own. Her hair was short and sort of fringed, framing her face in feathery layers that made her look a lot softer than he knew her to be. Her blue-green eyes were wary as she stepped up to his desk and held out her hand.

"Mr. Wolff."

He took her hand in his and disregarded the

flash of something hot and disconcerting that swept through him. This kind of thing was always happening if Kyra got too near—the perfect reason for keeping her at a distance. Not only wasn't she anywhere near his type, but an office affair could only get messy.

He saw a spurt of recognition pass across her eyes and disappear again just as quickly.

"Please, sit down." He waved a hand at the chair closest to her.

She did, but perched on the edge of the black leather seat, hands folded on her knees. Before he could speak, she started.

"If this is about my idea for the expansion division—"

"It's not." He cut her off, not wanting to discuss her plan.

His temper spiked as he remembered all of the half-baked ideas she'd come up with over the last year. Granted, one or two of them weren't bad. But she always had to push the envelope. Always had to go for just one more step.

And while a part of him admired her for the guts it took to rock the boat, a bigger part wanted to tell her that irritating people was *not* the fast track to success.

But then, he thought wryly, since the higher-ups had decided to promote her anyway...

She fidgeted in her chair, and Garrett brought his mind back to the task at hand. "According to your employee records, you're not due for another review until October, is that right?"

"Yeeessss." One word. At least five syllables.

He sensed her nervousness and did nothing to ease it. Her perfume, a subtle scent of flowers and citrus, drifted lazily to him and he frowned to himself as he tried to ignore it. Every time he saw her, that scent reached out for him, and he almost wondered if she used the stuff as some sort of feminine weapon. If so, it was a damn effective one.

Reaching for a manila file folder to his right, he opened it and laid it on his desk. Deliberately, he scanned the contents, though he'd already read the information it contained. She was nervous, and damned if some small part of him wasn't enjoying it. So many of the people in this company either admired her or were intimidated by her that he relished the chance to put her on edge a little.

She inched closer to the desk and strained to read her employee file upside down.

"If this is about the meeting with the Hartsfield people, I can assure you that I have the situation in hand," she said, shifting her gaze to him, and then back to the file, still open on his desk.

When he closed it, he saw the flash of irritation in her eyes, and enjoyed that, too.

"It's not."

"Then what?"

He leaned back in his chair, propped his elbows on the arms and steepled his fingertips together as he studied her. She was still nervous, but a flash of something mutinous darted through her eyes.

"I called you in here to let you know that you're going to be reviewed early next week."

Her blue-green eyes narrowed in suspicion. "My next review isn't due until October. Why now?"

He sat up, folded his arms atop the closed file and watched her. "I don't believe I'm required to give you a reason."

Kyra nodded shortly and felt her temper spike. The man was so calm, so controlled, she wanted to tear out her hair. There was something going on here, and she didn't have a clue what it was. Reviewed early meant one of two things: either she was going to be promoted—or fired.

Watching Garrett Wolff's closed expression didn't really give her any hints as to which way the wind was blowing on that score. But she had a pretty good idea where he would stand on the issue.

His pale blue eyes were steady on her and completely unreadable. It was as if that brief, electrical spark that had flashed between them hadn't even happened. Cold, she thought. He was cold, right down to the bone.

Too bad he looked so darn good. Garrett Wolff had blond hair that looked both too long and too tempting. He wore elegantly cut suits with the air of a pirate, and the swagger in his step was always just enough to make a woman either want to drool or kick him.

He was a presence at Voltage.

The bigwigs liked him. Trusted him.

Listened to him.

And he hated her.

She'd known that for months. Ever since she'd spoken up during a marketing meeting and said what everyone else had been thinking: that Garrett's ideas were outdated and too conservative.

Okay, she thought now, maybe not the best way to make a good impression on your boss. But she hadn't been trying to piss him off. Just make him see that she had good things to offer. That if given a chance, she could make a difference at Voltage.

Now it looked as though all she'd done was earn the enmity of the one person who could make or break her career.

Swell.

Well then, if she was already sinking, she might as well go for broke.

"Look, I know you don't like me—"

He cut her off. "This isn't personal, Ms. Fortune."

"The hell it isn't," she snapped, surging to her

feet as the tidal wave of anger carried her along in its wake. She was in this too deep now to start hedging her words or watching her step. Might as well be hanged for a lion as a lamb.

"Every time I make a suggestion for this company or take a stand against doing things the traditional way, you shoot me down."

He stood up, too, and towered over her. Not easy, since she was by no means a tiny little thing. It irritated her, having to tilt her head back to glare at him, but she managed.

"You don't make 'suggestions,' Kyra," he countered, through gritted teeth. "You torpedo other people's ideas and then try to ram your own through, with all the tact and sensitivity of a rampaging army."

"Is there something wrong with wanting to succeed?" She felt the temper bubbling inside her. Knew she should dial it down. Knew she should get a grip. But she just couldn't.

"Not as long as you don't eviscerate those who don't agree with you," he retorted, his eyes snapping now with a temper to match her own.

"You just don't want anyone rocking the boat," she challenged, planting her hands on the edge of his pristine desk and leaning toward him.

"And *you*," he declared, doing a little leaning of

his own, "don't have the patience to let things develop naturally."

"What good is patience?" Kyra lifted one hand and pushed back a fringe of hair that had drifted into her left eye. "While we're being patient, Fortune TX, Ltd. will sweep in and hustle off our major clients."

"They haven't yet," he reminded her.

"That's not to say they won't." Kyra stared him straight in the eye, unwilling now to back down from the precipice where her temper had carried her. "At Fortune, they're not afraid to take chances. To try something new. To foster their employees' imaginations."

"Then maybe you're working for the wrong company, Ms. *Fortune*."

She hissed in a breath. Ooh, that one hurt.

She pushed up from the desk. Folding her arms across her breasts, she concentrated for a full minute on inhaling and exhaling. She counted to ten. Then twenty. Then thirty.

Didn't work.

Still furious.

"Maybe you don't know this about me, Mr. Wolff, so let me be the first to tell you. I don't trade on my family name. It's for exactly that reason that I came to work for Voltage. I wanted to make it on my own talents. I've worked hard to earn my position here. And I'll work even harder until I have *your* job."

He snorted a derisive laugh that had Kyra's hackles lifting.

"Is that a threat, Ms. Fortune?"

"That's a promise, Mr. Wolff."

"I'll keep that in mind."

A tiny, tiny voice in the back of Kyra's brain was screeching, telling her that she was being an idiot. That she was risking everything she'd worked for by pissing off her boss.

But, she thought as she deliberately squashed that shrieking voice, at this point what did she have to lose? He already didn't like her. Maybe if he knew she was willing to stand up to him and fight for respect, he would, at least, admire her.

After several long seconds of silence ticked past, Kyra spoke again. "This review. You'll be doing it?"

He smiled again. "Yes."

A cold chill snaked along her spine. "I won't make it easy on you."

"What?"

"I know you want me fired."

He shook his head. "Contrary to what you believe, you don't actually know everything." He paused. "But the fact that you always act as if you do is irritating to some."

She squirmed uncomfortably.

"And I will say," he continued, "that maybe, Kyra, you've finally irritated the wrong people."

Another chill caught her and she stiffened. Lifting her chin high and squaring her shoulders, she nodded briskly. "Think whatever you want to think, Mr. Wolff. But I'm damn good at my job. And my record will speak for itself."

"We'll see, won't we?" he asked, and slowly sat down in his chair again. Picking up her employee file, he tucked it away in one of his desk drawers, then lifted his gaze to hers. "That's all for now. You can get back to work."

She opened her mouth to say something more, but shut it again almost instantly. She'd already said way too much. And knowing Garrett Wolff, he wouldn't forget a word of it.

Chapter 2

Kyra was still shaking as she left Garrett's office. She deliberately closed the door gently, wanting to kick herself for losing her temper. Hadn't she been told most of her life that her temper would only get her into trouble?

And for the most part, she reminded herself, she'd conquered that instinctive flash of anger that had prompted her into saying something she shouldn't too many times.

But that man, she thought grimly, could make a saint come storming out of heaven wielding thunderbolts.

"Are you all right, Ms. Fortune?"

Kyra's gaze snapped to Carol Summerhill, sitting at her desk. Short, with a lush figure, cropped, dark curly hair and a simpering smile that irritated everyone around her, with the exception of Garrett. Carol wouldn't see forty again, but she hid the signs of her age with perfectly applied makeup. And she guarded her boss's office with the zeal of a rabid dog.

"I'm just fine," Kyra managed to say through gritted teeth. "Thanks."

"I only wondered," Carol said slyly, "because you look a little…ill."

Only because that's how she was feeling. Along with terrified, furious and worried. But she'd be damned if she'd let Carol know that.

"No," she managed to answer, "I'm fine. Just a little warm. But thanks for your concern." Which was, Kyra knew, as much a lie as the answer she'd just given the woman.

Sucking in a gulp of air, she tried to steady the nerves jumping in the pit of her stomach. Then she forced a smile she didn't feel, and headed past Carol's desk. No way was she going to let the woman know just how shaken she really was.

The office door behind her opened abruptly, and Kyra spun around to face Garrett again.

"Still here, Ms. Fortune?" he inquired wryly, one eyebrow lifted into a high arch.

"Just leaving," she assured him.

"Good." Dismissing her, he turned to his assistant. "Carol, come inside and bring your pad."

"Yes, sir," she said, leaping to her feet like a dolphin breaching the surface of a pool to grab at a tasty fish.

The woman had absolutely no dignity, Kyra thought as she watched Garrett disappear back into the inner sanctum. She ground her teeth as Carol paused, gave her a slow smile and shut herself in their boss's office.

Kyra glared at the closed door and did the only thing she could in that situation. She stuck out her tongue, then left as quickly as possible.

The building was quiet, most of the employees having left for home long before. From down the hall came the soft drone of a vacuum cleaner, and outside the bank of windows behind Kyra's desk, rain spattered against the glass.

Oblivious to the faint background sounds, Kyra bent over the open file on her cluttered desktop. Frowning in concentration, she flipped through the pages of the Hartsfield report, making notations on the pad at her right. With no distractions, no interruptions, she'd have the presentation ready by morning.

If Garrett Wolff was really going to fire her, it wouldn't be because he'd found fault with her work.

A voice in the back of her mind muttered darkly about men with too much power. About the unfairness of it all. About how, despite how hard she tried, she would never really be good enough.

She swallowed and gripped her pen tightly in her fist. Whispers of self-doubt fluttered through her brain, but that was nothing new. Most of her life she'd covered up her fears with bravado. To the outside world, Kyra was a woman who knew exactly where she was going and just how to get there.

But inside, she was still the youngest child of a drunk. Unsure whom to trust. Unsure of her own abilities. Unsure of every damn thing.

"Okay," she said softly, as she mentally smoothed the knot of nerves in the pit of her stomach. "That's enough of that."

"Talking to yourself is not a good sign, you know."

Kyra jumped in her chair, slapped one hand to her chest and took a deep breath in an effort to nudge her heart down out of her throat. Her pulse beat wildly as her gaze shot to the man in the open doorway of her office.

Garrett Wolff stood there watching her. Well, he was leaning more than standing. One shoulder was braced against the doorjamb, one foot crossed over the other. His arms were folded across his chest and his sharp gaze was fixed on *her.* God knew how long he'd been there.

"Let me guess," she snapped, covering her own embarrassment with the familiar snarl of anger. "Instead of firing me, you decided to just scare me to death and save on the paperwork."

He grinned, and the solid punch of it raced across the room and hit Kyra like a bolt of something hot and dangerous.

Oh, *so* not good.

She'd known the man for eight years, during which time he'd irritated her, annoyed her and just plain pissed her off. But she'd never, ever felt a flash of desire for him. Okay, sure, she'd noticed how gorgeous he was.

Heck, she'd have had to be blind to have missed that.

But noticing and *noticing* were two different things.

Shaking his head, he unfolded his arms and shoved his hands into his pants pockets. "It's eleven o'clock at night, Ms. Fortune. Why are you still here?"

Uncomfortable under that cool, steady stare, she shifted a little in her seat. She'd thought she was alone in the building. Well, except for the cleaning crew and the security guards.

She often stayed late at night, to catch up on work,

to get a jump on the next day's tasks. She liked the quiet. Probably a holdover from living in a too-crowded house when she was a kid. Just remembering her father's sudden, unpredictable shouting rages could make her long for peace and quiet. But it was even more than that.

She liked knowing that she was alone and for a few hours could drop the pretense of always being in charge. Kyra knew darn well that most of her co-workers considered her an arrogant know-it-all.

Which would have been funny if it didn't bother her so much. God, she wished she *were* a know-it-all. School had never come easy to her. She'd always had to study twice as hard as anyone else to get the grades that had assured her of four years at Texas A&M.

And she'd worked even harder here at Voltage. Staring at Garrett now, though, Kyra wondered if all of her hard work had been for nothing. Frustrating to know that no matter how good her job performance, she could lose everything she'd been working toward because one man didn't like her.

Well, she wouldn't make it easy on him.

He was watching her now, still waiting for an answer to his question. "I'm just working out a few details in the Hartsfield plan."

One of his brows lifted. "Then you've managed to sign them on with Voltage?"

"Not yet," she admitted, wishing she could say yes. "But soon."

He nodded and straightened up, taking one or two steps into her office. "Good. But you don't have to work twenty-four hours a day, you know. Voltage really doesn't expect that of its employees."

It was strange, having him here in her office. As far as she could remember, this was his first visit. And since she knew full well that her career was currently dangling by a thread, she didn't count this as a social call.

Which meant he had another reason altogether for dropping by in the middle of the night.

She only wished she knew what it was.

"Really?" she countered, tilting her head to one side and studying him as he walked the perimeter of her office. "Then why are *you* still here?"

"Touché." He walked slowly around the room, examining the paintings on the wall, checking out the crystal vase of yellow roses on the credenza, and then finally stopping beside her desk.

He was too close for comfort. Kyra pushed her chair back from her desk so that she could give herself an extra foot or so of space and have an unobstructed view of the man.

His gaze locked on the night beyond the rain-spattered windows. Kyra waited, stubbornly refusing to be the first one to break the silence that seemed to stretch tautly between them. At last she was rewarded.

He turned his head to look at her. "Why are you so driven?"

She blinked, surprised not only by the question, but by the genuine curiosity she heard in his deep voice. There were, of course, lots of answers to the query, none of which she was interested in sharing with her boss.

Especially a boss who made no secret of the fact that he didn't much like her. But she had to say something.

"Why is it when a woman works hard, she's driven. When a man does the same thing, he's just conscientious?"

The smile that curved his lips suddenly was gone almost before it was born, but in that instant something warm and liquid rushed through Kyra, despite her efforts to stop it.

"Good point," he acknowledged. "But that doesn't answer the question."

"Why do you care about the answer?"

"Call it professional curiosity," he said with a slight shrug. "I see a young woman who should be out having a good time, and instead, she stays locked up in her office nearly every night."

"And you know this how?"

His lips twitched. "I'm the boss. I'm supposed to know these things."

He was keeping track of her? She didn't know what to think about that. Was that a good thing or a bad thing?

"I'd like to point out," she said cautiously, "that you're here in the middle of the night, too."

"Yeah," he said, turning his gaze back to the windows, When he continued, his voice was lower, more thoughtful. "But spending my nights in this building wasn't something I planned."

"So go home."

He turned his head to look at her again, and Kyra saw a half smile flash across his face before it disappeared again. "Good idea. How about we both go?"

He was being nice.

Why?

That swirl of emotion started in the bottom of her stomach again. Surprise flickered through her as she realized she was actually enjoying the sensation. There was something very…intimate about being here in the office alone with him. With the stormy night crouched outside and only a puddle of light from the lamp on her desk illuminating the room, it was as if they were the only two people in the world.

His presence seemed to make the room shrink in size. The walls seemed to close in around them.

The tap of rain against the windowpanes was a steady, almost musical accompaniment to the silence stretching between them. She looked into his blue eyes and— Kyra caught herself and shook her head.

If Garrett was being nice, it was only to lull her into complacency before putting her head on the chopping block.

"I'm just going to finish up this last report," she said, "and then—"

"Mr. Wolff?"

They both looked toward the doorway. Carol Summerhill stood there, watching them in obvious disapproval. Her eyes were narrowed and her lips were nothing more than a flat, grim line.

Kyra suddenly felt like a cheating wife caught sneaking out of a cheap motel. Stupid, she knew. But the look on Carol's face was that of a jealous woman. Weird.

Garrett, though, seemed more annoyed at the interruption than anything else. "Yes, Carol?"

The woman shifted her gaze from Kyra to their boss. "I only wanted to remind you that you have a teleconference at six in the morning."

"Thank you."

His tone, if not the words themselves, were dismissive, but Carol ignored both. "I'll walk out with you if you like."

Geez, Kyra thought. Had the woman brought rose petals to toss down in front of him, too?

Garrett stiffened. "No, thanks. You go ahead."

"Oh."

Carol looked stupefied, as if she couldn't quite believe he'd chosen to remain and talk to Kyra rather than leave with her. Well, heck. Kyra was pretty surprised at that herself.

"I have a few things I need to discuss with Ms. Fortune," Garrett said.

"I see." Clearly, Carol didn't see and wasn't at all happy about it, either. But left with no other choice, she backed out and said, "I'll see you in the morning, then."

"Fine."

When they were alone again, Kyra chanced a look at Garrett. And she had to ask. "Do you really enjoy all the hero worship?"

He frowned at her. "What?"

She waved one hand at the empty doorway, then stood up to face him, feeling more in charge on her feet. "Carol. Your guard dog."

He laughed shortly and the sound surprised Kyra. But the *real* surprise was suddenly realizing that he was even better-looking when he smiled.

Oh dear God.

Stop noticing these things, she told herself.

Shaking his head, he strolled slowly around her

desk, idly lifting first her brass nameplate, then a framed picture of her and her brothers and sister. He held the photo and studied it as he spoke. "Carol's been with me for ten years and she's…territorial."

"Yeah," Kyra said. "Like a Doberman."

"What do you mean?" Still holding the photo, he shot her a glance.

"Only that it's probably easier to get an audience with the Pope than it is to get in and see you."

Frowning slightly, he said, "I didn't realize."

Maybe he really didn't know how well Carol protected him from the people who worked for him. Maybe he was totally unaware that his assistant practically threw herself in front of his door to keep the unwashed at bay. But if he didn't know, he darn well should.

"You ought to get out more, General," Kyra told him. "Visit with the troops."

Thoughtfully, he nodded. "Maybe you're right." Then he shifted his gaze back to the picture he still held. "Your family?"

"Yes." She didn't have to look at the photo to know what he was seeing. A few months ago she and her siblings had gotten together for lunch, and Kyra had asked a waiter to take their picture. It wasn't often anymore that she, Susan, Vincent and Daniel were in the same place at the same time. Though they hadn't exactly been close when they were kids, in the last few years they'd all done some reaching out.

And to be honest, it was Kyra who'd had to do the most reaching. As the youngest of the four, she'd been the most removed from everyone's lives. And thanks to Vincent running interference between her and her father, she had never really suffered the man's rages as her brothers and sister had.

In the last few months, things had really changed for Leonard Fortune's kids, too. Susan, Daniel and even Vincent had found love and happiness. They all felt a sense of peace they'd never had before.

God knew, they'd all earned it. Growing up as the children of Leonard Fortune hadn't exactly been a game plan for success.

As the youngest, Kyra had been spoiled by her mother and protected from her father's drunken rages by Vincent's stubborn determination. Kyra'd been spared most of the misery her siblings had survived. But they were all grown up now. Succeeding on their own terms. Making lives for themselves, despite their father. Despite everything.

And Kyra was determined to do no less than her brothers and sister had done. She had every intention of making a success of her career and then somehow finding the love she'd always dreamed about.

Garrett continued to assess the photo. "Big family."

"Four kids is a lot, I guess."

"I'm an only child," he said, and set the frame gingerly down on her desk, turning it back toward her with the tip of one finger.

"Must have been…quiet," she said, not sure what he was getting at. Not sure why he was still here, in her office, talking to her as if they were old friends. Or lovers.

Her brain fizzled at the thought and she was forced to remind herself again that noticing Garrett Wolff as anything other than her boss was a one-way ticket to trouble.

He shoved both hands into his pockets. "Too quiet, sometimes."

Now what did that mean?

As if suddenly realizing he'd said too much, he pulled his hands from his pockets, checked his watch and said, "I'm going home. I suggest you do the same, Ms. Fortune. The work will still be here tomorrow."

Unable to help herself, she said, "Yes. But will I?"

He studied her for a long minute and shook his head. "Your review's not till next week, remember? And besides, why are you so sure you're going to be fired?"

She swallowed hard. "Because I know what you think of me."

One corner of his mouth lifted. "You can't possibly know everything, Ms. Fortune. But the fact that you always act as if you do can be irritating."

Instinctively, she tried to argue that point. "I don't—"

"Who knows?" he added. "Maybe this time you really have irritated the wrong people."

Kyra felt cold right down to the bone. Gone was the Mr. Nice Guy, chitchatting at night with one of the lesser beings. And in his place was the boss she'd come to know so well. Mr. Ice.

"I won't make it easy on you," she said, feeling it was only fair to warn the man that she wouldn't give up without a fight.

"Ms. Fortune," he said, "you never do anything the easy way."

Chapter 3

Two days later, Garrett was beginning to see what Kyra was talking about.

Walking through the expansion division—hell, *his* division, he'd already noticed people staring at him as if he were an apparition. Some looked nervous, as if he were there to lop off heads or personally hand out pink slips. Others were simply too stunned to return a simple greeting when he smiled and said good morning. And a couple of people paid no attention to him at all, leaving him to wonder if they even knew who the hell he was.

Irritation bubbled inside him. Damn it, he hated to admit that Kyra Fortune was right. But now that he was actually noticing what was going on outside the walls of his own office, he was forced to. Carol had always been so efficient, so on top of everything, he'd never really noticed how much of his world she ran.

Garrett was annoyed to have to acknowledge that Kyra Fortune had seen something he'd missed.

Muted sunlight streamed through the tinted windows surrounding the busy floor. At tiny cubicles and paper-cluttered desks, people hunched over their work or answered the ringing phones. Piped-in music battled for precedence over the sounds of people talking and typing.

And as he walked through it all, he realized he was just another distraction.

Damn it, he *had* been locked away too long. He'd lost touch with his team.

Oh, he met with a select few once a week, but the men and women who manned the glass cubicles sprawled across the steel-gray carpet were strangers to him. And he couldn't understand how he'd let that happen.

He hadn't set out to be alone in an ivory tower. But that was exactly where he was.

Now all he had to do was figure out how to change things.

"C'mon, Kyra, let it go for awhile. Relax. Have a drink. Dance."

Kyra sighed, picked up her margarita and looked

over the rim of the glass at her friend, Isabella San-chez. Isa's long, dark hair was a riot of curls around her pretty face. Her dark brown eyes were big and expressive, and her full mouth was turned up in a teasing smile.

But tonight not even her best friend could wangle an answering smile out of Kyra. "I'm just not in the mood, Isa. I shouldn't have come out tonight. I'm only going to be a supreme downer." She shook her head, set her glass on the scarred tabletop and leaned back in her chair.

"Girl, you're letting him win."

"He's going to win anyway," Kyra muttered, straightening up at the mere reference to Garrett Wolff. She'd already told Isa about the confronta-tion with her boss two days ago. And because she was a great friend, she'd promptly insisted on taking Kyra out to unwind.

Too bad it wasn't working.

Not even the atmosphere of Rio's, an upscale bar and restaurant, was enough to lift Kyra's black mood. All around them people sat at round tables dotting the gleaming wood floor. Iron wall sconces shone with soft light, as did the cream-colored glass balls that hung on silver chains draped from beams in the ceiling.

Cocktail waitresses in black shorts and yellow T-shirts dipped and swayed as they moved through the crowd, carrying loaded trays of drinks and nachos. In the far corner a country and western band swung into a fast-tempo tune that had couples streaming toward the large square dance floor.

Against one wall a long, intricately carved mahogany bar was manned by three bartenders hustling to keep up with demand. A wall of mirrors backed the bar and reflected the room, so that it seemed to go on forever.

Isa reached across the table and patted Kyra's hand. "Don't let him get to you like this."

"Can't help it," she admitted, and dragged one fingernail through the circle of water left by her glass on the tabletop. Staring blindly at the path of her scarlet nail, she muttered, "He's going to fire me."

"You don't know that."

She laughed shortly, despite the sinking sensation inside. "Sure I do." Reaching out, she snagged a tortilla chip, then sat back in her chair and nibbled it. "He's hated me since day one."

"You don't know that, either."

"Please. He ignores me in meetings and practically runs the other way if he happens to see me in a hallway."

"Hmm…" Isa smiled, took a sip of her drink and set it down again.

"What's that supposed to mean?"

Her best friend shrugged and smiled. "Just hmm…"

"There's more."

"I'm only thinking that maybe he's not avoiding you because he hates you, but because he's attracted to you."

Kyra choked on a piece of chip. Coughing wildly, she held up one hand, grabbed her margarita and took a gulp. Still choking, eyes watering, she stared at the other woman. "Are you nuts?"

Laughing now, Isa shook her head and winked at a nearby man when he turned to look at her. Then, focusing on Kyra again, she said, "Sexual tension can erupt in the weirdest places."

Kyra felt a rush shoot straight through her. Her friend's words echoed over and over in her mind, and Kyra tried, desperately, to think about them objectively. But there was just no way.

"This isn't about sexual tension," she snapped, then winced and lowered her voice as she leaned across the table. "Trust me when I say neither one of us is feeling anything like that."

"Uh-huh."

Disbelief rang in Isa's tone, and Kyra didn't know how to convince her friend. Especially when there was a slim, fragile, wispy, almost nonexistent thread of worry unspooling inside her. Fine. Garrett was gorgeous. And just maybe, under other, very different circumstances, there might have been something between them.

In a different life.

On a different planet.

In another universe.

Oh, boy.

"I see that look," Isa said with an air of triumph.

"What look?"

"The look that says, 'I might be interested.'"

"I'm not."

"Sure."

"And even if I were," Kyra hedged, "he isn't."

"Okay."

"Stop agreeing with me."

"Whatever you say."

Kyra's eyes narrowed. "You're doing this deliberately."

"Yeah," Isa said, laughing. "But it got your mind off everything else, didn't it?"

Yes, it had. However, her mind was probably safer worrying about being fired than it was thinking about Garrett Wolff in a sexual way. She'd spent the last two days waiting for the other shoe to drop. She'd half expected to be called into his office for the review he'd promised her and then be given a hearty handshake and a severance check.

Her nerves were stretched tight and every breath felt like an Olympic event. She couldn't take much more of this. Plus, Garrett had been acting differently the last couple of days, too. He'd come out of his office and strolled through the division often enough to start making *other* people nervous. All of a sudden he was paying attention. Talking to people. Listening to people.

And none of that could be good.

There was something else going on here. Something he was planning.

She just wished she knew what it was.

"You're thinking again," Isa said, reaching across the table to slap Kyra's shoulder. "Cut it out."

"Okay, okay." Shaking her head, she took a deep breath, blew it out and said, "You're right. No more thinking about Garrett Wolff. No more thinking about work. What's the point, right?"

"Right."

"I mean, if I'm going to be fired, thinking about it won't change anything, right?"

"Right." Isa nodded and gave her an encouraging grin.

"And if I'm living out of a shopping cart by this time next month, I'll survive, right?"

Isa laughed outright. "You really should have gone for a drama degree instead of business."

"Fine, fine." She picked up her margarita for another sip, then smiled as she set it down. "No drama. No thinking."

"Atta girl."

Across the room, the band launched into a fast-paced song with a pounding, staccato rhythm that had even Kyra's toes tapping.

"Come on," Isa said, standing up and grinning. "It's a line dance. Let's go."

She thought about it for a second or two. She hadn't been in the mood for company tonight. Hadn't wanted to come out and join the world. She'd wanted nothing more than to curl up in the dark quiet of her condo and concentrate on the misery being heaped on her.

But now that she was here, the world was looking a little friendlier. She wasn't sure if it was Isa's influence or the margarita, but whatever it was, it beat the heck out of sitting home alone, brooding.

Jumping to her feet, Kyra said, "Good idea." If she was dancing, she wouldn't be thinking. And right now that sounded like a plan.

She followed Isa through the crowd and took her place in the long line of dancers already moving through an intricate ten-step routine. Kyra swung her hair out of her eyes, laughed aloud and slid into the moves with practiced ease, letting go of everything in the sheer enjoyment of the music washing over her.

Boots stomped against the floor, hands clapped,

dancers shouted and the band played faster, challenging them all to increase the pace.

Garrett stood at the edge of the dance floor and watched Kyra move. And damn, the woman had some great moves.

She wore a long-sleeved, red silk blouse, dark blue jeans that clung to her shapely legs like a lover's hands, and shiny black boots. Her hips swayed with the beat and her feet flew, keeping up with the complicated steps of the dance. He watched her toss her head back and laugh, and he was caught by the way her eyes shone and her whole face lit up with pleasure.

He'd never seen Kyra like this.

Always, at the office, she was the career-committed female, on the way up. She was good at her job and concentrated on the work. She was usually pleasant, always efficient and completely annoying. And still he'd noticed her.

Hadn't wanted to, but how could he have helped it? Any man would have been drawn to the scent of her. The look of her, softly feminine in slacks and jackets that looked as if they'd been designed especially for her.

At Voltage, she was an irritant who touched him in ways he didn't like to think about.

But here at Rio's she was someone else entirely.

And something inside him tightened into a knot of hunger so raw, so strong, it surprised even him.

He'd only dropped by the club to see the owner, an old friend from college. But he'd been trapped there the moment he saw Kyra headed for the dance floor.

As the song ended, the band jumped quickly into another, not wanting to lose the crowd up dancing. Kyra and the dark-haired woman she was talking to automatically started moving again, keeping their places in the long line of dancers.

And almost before Garrett knew it, he was stepping up beside the tall blonde with the beautiful eyes.

She laughed, spun, kicked her right heel, then looked up at him, and all semblance of joy drained from her face. Her shining eyes went flat and cool and suspicious.

He was surprised to realize he didn't like the fact she was so upset at running into him.

"Ms. Fortune," he said, speaking loud enough to be heard over the band.

"Mr. Wolff," she muttered, then started backing off the floor.

Damn it. She couldn't get away fast enough. He never should have talked to her. Should have just left. But how the hell could he have done that after seeing her smile? Laugh? Dance? "Going somewhere?" he asked.

"I'm tired."

"You don't look tired." Just eager to escape.

She blew out a disgusted breath that ruffled the fringe of bangs on her forehead. "You know, we're not at the office. I don't *have* to talk to you."

That stung. And that fact, too, surprised the hell out of him. He scrubbed the back of his neck. "We're not at the office, so why don't you drop the attitude?"

Her head snapped back and her blue-green eyes shot sparks. "If you don't like my attitude, why are you talking to me?"

"Seemed like a good idea at the time," he muttered, though at the moment he was having a hard time remembering just why he'd followed his instinct to approach her. Then his gaze dropped, and he looked her up and down slowly, and he remembered.

This was a different Kyra from the one he knew, and damned if she didn't appeal to him on all sorts of levels.

Another dancer bumped into her, and Garrett reached out to steady her. At the slight contact, heat swept up his arm and ricocheted around his chest. She sucked in a breath and shook herself loose from his grasp. But her eyes glistened and her face was flushed.

"Kyra," the pretty brunette shouted from close by. "Everything okay?"

"Fine." She waved a hand at her friend, then shifted her gaze back to Garrett. "If you'll excuse me—"

She was leaving, and suddenly he didn't want her to go. "Not afraid, are you?"

She stiffened and he could almost see her temper spike.

"Of you?"

"That's the question."

She snorted. "Hardly."

"Then stay," he said, holding out one hand. "Dance."

She looked from his eyes to his hand and back again. "Why should I?"

He shrugged. "Music's too good to waste?"

Her lips twitched and she looked at him with something a little closer to curiosity than animosity.

"Good point."

"And hey," he said, pushing the small advantage he seemed to have, "there's always the chance that you'll dance me into the ground."

"There is that."

"A *small* chance."

"We'll see about that." She grabbed his hand and let him pull her back onto the dance floor. Then she took her place in line and fell into the steps of the dance as if it was instinctive.

Garrett couldn't keep up.

But then, it was hard to remember dance steps when your gaze was locked on a particular woman's behind and how it swayed in time to the music. Every cell in his body felt as if it were boiling. He didn't care about the damn dance. He'd only wanted to prolong this moment with Kyra. There was something about her. Something that was beginning to resonate inside him. Something he really didn't want to examine too closely.

Kyra stumbled slightly, but caught herself quickly and hoped no one else had noticed. She felt clumsy, awkward.

And it was all Garrett Wolff's fault.

He'd surprised her, showing up at Rio's.

Astonished her by wanting to dance.

And was now busy confusing the hell out of her by watching her so closely. She felt his gaze on her as surely as she would have his touch. Heat simmered deep inside her and made her long for the cool night air.

But there was no escaping Garrett's company. Not unless she was willing to let him think he'd chased her off. And she wouldn't give him that satisfaction.

As her brain raced and her feet struggled to keep

up with the dance, the song ended and the band moved instantly into something slower, softer. The fiddle player moved to the front of the stage and scraped his bow across the instrument's strings. A haunting melody seeped into the room and the crowd quieted as the lead singer's voice quietly sang of love lost.

Kyra backed up, trying not to look at Garrett at all. Isa slipped away into the crowd, and Kyra was alone with the man who held the future of her career in his hands.

"Dance with me," he said softly as more of the line dancers faded back into the crowd.

"I just did," she said, despite the knot lodged in her throat.

"Kyra..." His gaze moved over her face, studying her as if seeing her for the first time. Holding out one hand to her, he said again, "Dance with me."

Around them, the music swelled, the strains of the fiddle an aching, living thing in the air.

And Kyra took his hand, stepping in close to him.

She couldn't say why. She knew she shouldn't. Knew it would be better for both of them if she simply went back to her table with Isa and forgot all about running into Garrett. But she couldn't do it. Caught by something dark and dangerous glittering in his pale blue eyes, she followed a stronger instinct than the one telling her to leave.

He held her right hand in his left, wrapped his right arm around her waist and pulled her close to him. The scent of him invaded her, making her head swim. The strength of his grip made her pulse jump. The feel of his thighs moving against hers had her closing her eyes and resting her head on his shoulder.

Her heartbeat quickened and something hot and thick moved through her veins.

Music filled the air and swept through her senses, making everything seem sharper, clearer, hotter. She felt as if she were quivering, poised on the very lip of a precipice. But she couldn't see the edge of the cliff and didn't know what waited for her at the bottom.

All she knew for sure was her life had just taken another turn for the weird.

Chapter 4

The music stopped, then started again with a pulse-pounding, foot-stomping beat.

And still Garrett couldn't let Kyra go. She felt good in his arms. Too good. It wasn't something he'd expected, but now that he'd found it, damned if he didn't want to hold on to the feeling.

She stared up at him, ignoring the other dancers, as he was. Her eyes looked more green than blue in the dim light of the club, and he felt, as well as saw, the flicker of something warm and intriguing in their depths.

All around them, dancers moved to the beat while the two of them stood, gazes locked, oblivious to everyone else. His chest tight, Garrett fought for breath and told himself to let her go. To step back before he did something that neither of them would be happy about.

But Kyra moved first.

"Thanks," she said, sliding her hand from his and stepping out of his embrace. "For the dance, I mean," she added quickly.

His hands felt empty, and he rubbed the tips of his fingers together as if trying to find the warmth that had slipped away so suddenly.

"Right." Nodding, he stepped off the dance floor and waited for her to follow. Once clear of the dozens of couples dancing the Cotton-eyed Joe, Garrett scrubbed one hand across his face and tried to find a way out of this now uncomfortable situation.

What the hell had he been thinking?

Dancing with Kyra Fortune?

Letting himself imagine doing a hell of a lot more with her?

Where was this coming from? He'd never known a woman who irritated him more than Kyra. She was opinionated, pushy, arrogant and an all-around thorn in his side.

So why did he suddenly want to grab her and kiss her blind?

"Look," she said, pulling Garrett from the wild

thoughts racing through his mind, "I'm going to go back and join my friend—"

"Yeah," he said, grabbing at the excuse she'd offered. "And I've got to go—"

"—so how about we just pretend this never happened?"

"Huh?" Surprised, he stared at her. Her gaze flicked to each side of her, as if making sure no one was listening. When she looked back at him, her eyes were clear and cool, with no hint of the spark he'd seen earlier.

She blew out a breath. "It was a nice dance, but seriously, it was just a fluke, right? I mean, I was here, you were here…."

He nodded. "Coincidence."

"Exactly." She beamed at him as if he were an especially slow student who'd finally caught on to the day's lesson. "So all I'm saying is that there's no point in making a big deal out of this."

Made perfect sense, he told himself. It was the out he should have been looking for. So why, he wondered, was he feeling the first stirrings of anger inside him? He was already regretting dancing with her. Why in the hell should he be pissed because she was asking him to forget about the whole thing? That ripple of anger spread and bubbled throughout his body, and he almost welcomed it. Heaven knew it was a far more familiar feeling around Kyra than anything else he'd been experiencing that night. "So we just ignore it."

"How hard can it be?"

"Getting easier every second."

She frowned. "No reason to get cranky. I'm doing this for both of us."

He folded both arms across his chest and braced his feet far apart in an unconscious fighting stance. "Thanks so much."

"You know," she said, giving in to a bit of anger herself, "I think I'm being reasonable about all of this. I'm just saying what you're thinking."

"Wow. A mind reader, too. I had no idea you were a part-time mystic."

Her jaw worked as if she were biting her tongue. Hard. She leaned in toward him, captured his gaze with hers. "I don't know why *you* get to act all huffy. This is all *your* fault."

"What?"

"Hey, I didn't ask you to dance."

Good point. She hadn't even known he was in the building. If he'd just slipped out the front door instead of following her to the dance floor, none of this would be happening. Disgusted with himself, he felt his battle stance dissolve, and he shoved both hands into his jeans pockets. "If I could kick my own ass right now, believe me, I'd do it."

Her lips twitched and he found himself staring at her mouth and wondering how it would taste.

Damn it.

"So you agree?" she asked.

Though it cost him dearly to agree with Kyra Fortune about anything, he had to admit she had the right idea here. To just forget about this little blip in their relationship. To put them both back on an even footing. Even if that meant making them armed adversaries again. They were much safer that way.

"Yes." He gritted his teeth, determined now to just get away from her as fast as he could.

"Good." She nodded abruptly, but didn't move to leave.

"Something else?" he asked, pitching his voice to be heard above the music.

She looked as though she wanted to say something, then thought better of it. "No. I mean… No."

"Okay." He glanced at his watch, more for effect than anything else. "I've got an appointment so—"

"Oh." A flash of something that might have been disappointment streaked across her features and was gone again in an instant. Then she lifted her chin, looked him in the eye and said, "All right. Then, goodbye."

"Yeah." Why wasn't he moving?

"See you at work."

"Right." He still didn't budge. For God's sake, he told himself, move.

Before he could, though, she turned and walked away, weaving through the crowd with a lazy grace that held Garrett captivated. Even after the mob of people swallowed her, he stared after her, like some lovesick schoolboy hoping for another smile from the head cheerleader.

He shook his head as if trying to shake Kyra out of his mind. But as he turned and stalked toward the front door, storming through the crowd like a man possessed, he already knew it wouldn't be that easy.

He'd held her now.

He knew what she felt like in his arms.

And he wondered why in the hell the first woman to stir his senses in years had to be the one woman who made a habit out of making his life miserable.

It appeared that Fate really did have a sense of humor.

A twisted one.

"What the heck was *that* about?" Isa demanded as soon as Kyra made it back to their table.

She dropped into a chair, slapped one hand to her spinning stomach and reached for her margarita before she tried to answer her best friend. While the icy slush slid down her throat, Kyra tried to get a grip on the different feelings racing through her.

But she just couldn't do it.

Finally, she lifted her gaze to her friend's. "I have absolutely no idea."

Isa shook her head. "Not buying it, girlfriend," she said flatly. "There is something going on between you two."

"He's my *boss.*" Oh God, she'd danced with her boss. She'd gotten all hot and squishy while pressed up against Garrett Wolff. Kyra propped her elbows on the table and cupped her face in her hands. "This is so not good."

Isabella laughed, clearly enjoying herself. "Yes it is. God, Kyra, you've been so tightly wrapped the last few years, you might as well have been vacuum packed. It's more than time that you cut loose a little."

Kyra lifted her head and glared at her friend. "Not with *him.*"

"That wasn't how it looked to me."

"Don't you get it, Isa? The man holds my career in his tight fist. One word from him and I'm finished."

"Looked to me like he was thinking more about starting than finishing," Isa said.

"Yeah, but starting what? An affair?" Kyra groaned again. "God, that sounds so cheesy."

"But interesting, right?" Isa leaned on the table, crossing her arms on the glossy surface. "I mean, there was definitely some sparkage, right?"

"Boy howdy."

"Excellent."

"Not excellent," Kyra protested, though not quite as strongly as she should have.

An affair with Garrett Wolff would be disastrous—and fabulous. Terrifying—and exciting.

"It doesn't have to be the end of the world, Kyra."

"Yeah, but it could be," she said, then added, "and I can't risk it. Can't take the chance of putting my career on the line. I can't fail, Isa. I owe my family that."

Isa had heard this before, so she leaned back in her chair and shook her head slowly. "You're always thinking you owe something to somebody. So my question is, what do you owe yourself, Kyra? When do you get to do something just for you?"

Good question.

Kyra only wished she had an answer.

Ryan Fortune drew in a long, shuddering breath and wondered how much longer he'd be able to accomplish that simple task.

His body was shutting down. He felt it. The invader in his brain was winning the battle. He knew with a bone-deep certainty that there were only a handful of days left to him. If that.

Lying against a stack of plump pillows, he shifted slightly in his bed, pleased to feel muscles respond to thought. Such a simple thing, really. To stretch. To feel the play of muscle and bone.

To live.

He stared up at the ceiling and watched the dance of sunlight and shadow across the pale surface. He felt the soft breeze slipping through the partially opened window, and he could smell spring on the wind. Through the open curtains, he saw the trees outside his bedroom, budding now after a cold, hard winter.

He wished to hell he could be around to enjoy another spring. To curse another summer heat wave. Enjoy another Christmas. Hell, to do something as simple as walk the land, Lily's hand firmly clasped in his.

Frustration bubbled inside. His whole damn life he'd been a doer. He'd never been one to sit when he could stand, walk when he could run. He liked being in the thick of things. Holding out a hand to help those behind, while always reaching forward.

He'd built a proud family. He'd increased the legacy left by his own father, and knew that his children would do the same.

And still it wasn't enough.

He wasn't ready to go. At sixty, he should have lots of years left. He should be able to sit on a damn rocking chair on the front porch of the Double

Crown and watch his great-grandchildren playing in the sun.

Hell, only a year ago he'd had grand dreams and plans, and now…he only wished he and Lily could stop and watch a sunset together again. He wished he had the strength to run his fingers through her hair, to kiss her, to make love to her one more time.

Ryan's eyes closed and a soft smile crossed his face as he remembered what his daddy used to say. If wishes were horses, beggars would ride.

"You're right, Dad," he whispered, as if Kingston Fortune were there in the room with him. Who knew, maybe his spirit was there, getting ready to escort Ryan's soul on its trip to…wherever.

Funny. His mind kept drifting. Never used to be like that. Used to be able to concentrate. Focus. Now… "No more wishing," he whispered into the silence of his room. "Instead, I'll just remember what I've had." More than most, that was for damn certain, he assured himself.

He'd loved and been loved by two women in his life. He'd raised children and known the love of family, which when you came right down to it, was all that meant anything.

He frowned and gave a short sigh—all he could spare. He'd made mistakes; all men did. He regretted some, but others had caused good things to happen in the end, so it was hard to be sorry about them.

Still, he'd tried to do his best. Tried to make a difference—not only for his family, but for the world. He'd tried. Damn, he'd tried.

He only wished he knew if he'd succeeded.

"Ryan, honey?"

He opened his eyes and turned his head on the pillow, following the voice that he knew would be with him through eternity.

"Still beautiful," he whispered, and watched his wife's luscious mouth curve into a smile.

"Silly man," she said, and unnecessarily straightened the sheet and light blanket covering him. Smoothing, running her fingertips across the fine linen, she avoided looking at him.

She did that so often these last few days.

Ryan knew why. There would be tears in her amazing dark eyes. There were always tears now, and oh, how he wanted to be able to stop those tears for her. He wanted to grab her up, tumble her onto this wide, now lonely bed and bury his body deep within hers.

Strange how the hunger for life didn't ebb as death drew near.

In his mind, he was still the strong young man who'd seen a teenage Lily Redgrove and lost his heart. It didn't matter who or what had come between that time and this. There'd always been that slender thread connecting their two hearts. It had taken a lifetime for them to finally come together—and when they had it had been well worth the wait. But oh God, they were being cheated out of all the years to come.

"Stop," he whispered. "Sit."

She did, perching on the edge of the mattress as if she were a bird gingerly landing on a live electrical wire. "Do you want anything, honey? Can I get you something?"

"Time," he said, finding a smile for her. "Give me more time, Lily."

"We'll have time, honey. We will." She picked up his hand and held it gently between her own, as if she could somehow transfer her health, her vitality, to him.

Sunlight splashed across the big room and backlit Lily until her dark hair looked gilded. A strong woman, Lily. She'd been through a lot in her life and she'd never been broken. She'd faced up to tough situations and stood her ground. Yet now she was deliberately trying to pretend that the end wasn't staring them in the face.

And he'd gone along for the most part. He was tempted to continue to play the game they'd somehow slipped into. To keep pretending that this was nothing more than a bad case of flu. That he'd be back walking the land in a week or two.

God knew, pretense was more comforting than

truth. But there were a few things he needed to say to her, while he still could.

"Lily, honey…"

As if she could read his mind, she shook her head. "No, don't you start telling me goodbye, Ryan Fortune. Because I don't want to hear it. You're not going anywhere. You're not going to leave me. I won't allow it. You'll stay right here until *I* say different. You understand me?"

He chuckled, and the sensation rippled through his aching body like a fever. "You always were a bossy woman."

She sniffed, surreptitiously wiped her eyes with her fingertips, then smiled. "And you always were a smooth talker."

God, he'd loved her most of his life. Those dark, exotic eyes of hers. That smooth, caramel-colored skin, the thick, heavy black hair. The smile that lit up something inside him as if it were New Year's Eve in Times Square.

How hard it was to let her go.

"I want you to remember, always," he said, keeping his gaze locked with hers, "how much I love you."

She sucked in a gulp of air. "I know."

He nodded briefly. "Emmett's going to keep an eye on Linda, so don't you worry there."

"Yes, Ryan."

He smiled again. "I must really be sick for you to agree with me so easily."

"Damn you, Ryan, you're making me cry again."

He paid no attention. "And you make sure you get the children to help you out around here when I'm gone."

"You're not going any—"

"Lily, it's time to stop lying."

"I like the lies better," she admitted.

He gave her a half smile. "Hell, girl, so do I. But even I can't hold off death."

"You could if you tried. Damn it, Ryan, you're the most stubborn, hardheaded, just plain cussedly determined man I've ever known," she said, leaning down until her mouth was just a breath away from his. "Fight this. For me. For us."

He gave her hand a squeeze, no more than a touch of his flesh to hers. "I'm tired, Lily. I don't want to leave you, but I'm tired."

Her dark eyes filled with the tears she'd been holding back for so many days. And this time she let them fall. Leaning her forehead against his, she said softly, "You are the love of my life, Ryan Fortune. Always and forever you will be with me."

"Always and forever," he repeated, then pressed this moment, this sun-washed moment of time with Lily, into his mind so that when he got wherever he was going she would be there with him.

Then his wife lay down beside him, curling into him, and Ryan Fortune counted his blessings again.

"He's waiting for you."

"Thanks." Kyra walked into Garrett's office without even looking at Carol. It took a heck of a lot of nerve, since the woman had a stare that always made her feel like a bug being pinned to a board.

Kyra opened the door and paused, since the great man himself was on the phone. He glanced up, waved her in, but continued his conversation.

Kyra closed the door behind her and stood uncertainly where she was. Moving closer would look as though she were trying to listen in on his phone call.

Weird, she thought. Yes, they'd agreed to forget all about the whole dancing thing. But being here in the office with him, while the memory of his arms around her was still so clear, was harder than she'd thought it would be.

Of course, she admitted silently, she'd proposed the whole "ignore the situation" thing *before* she'd spent the night tossing and turning. Her dreams had been filled with Garrett Wolff.

And in those dreams they hadn't been dancing.

Heat rushed up to fill her cheeks, and she quickly turned her face away, making a big production out of studying a terribly silly still life, framed and hanging on his wall. Funny, she'd never noticed it before.

Now that she had, she couldn't imagine why a man like Garrett would have hung a painting of a sick-looking pear beside a half-eaten apple and called it art.

Whatever the reason, the painting had at least distracted her from revisiting last night's dreams, where a very naked, very talented Garrett had made her body buzz and her mind explode.

Dangerous territory, she warned herself, and turned back around to look at him again. Seated behind his desk, Garrett looked every inch the polished executive. His dark blue pin-striped suit was cut to perfection. He also wore a stark white shirt and a silk tie the same pale blue as his eyes.

Oh, boy.

"Yes, sir, I understand," Garrett was saying as he made notes on a yellow legal pad. "I'm sure we can handle it within a couple of days. Yes."

He glanced at her and Kyra straightened up.

"Ms. Fortune is here right now. Yes, I'll take care of it."

Oh, God.

Sexual fantasies flew out the window as a sense of dread curled in the pit of her stomach.

Was this it?

Was the boom about to be lowered?

She squeezed her eyes shut briefly. Man. One

dance with him and he fires her. What would he have done if they'd actually slept together?

Kyra swallowed back the panic scratching at her throat. Her stomach spun and her hands went damp.

He hung up the phone, stood up behind his desk and looked at her through pale, disinterested eyes. It was as if the man from the night before—the one who'd danced with her, held her, then starred in an X-rated dream sequence—had never existed.

It was for the best, she told herself firmly, though a huge part of her wasn't buying it.

"You sent for me?" she asked, prepared to take whatever he had to dish out.

"Yes." Garrett tossed his pen onto his desktop, swept back the edges of his suit coat and shoved both hands into the pockets of his slacks. "Go home and pack a bag, Ms. Fortune. You and I leave for a conference in Colorado in two hours."

"Conference?"

"Yes."

"You and I?"

"Is there an echo in here I'm unaware of?"

"No." She spoke up quickly and felt the knot of unease in her stomach slowly unwind. But in its place was a thread of curiosity. Why her? Why now? She wasn't usually assigned to out of town meetings. "I was just—"

"I'll fill you in on the way," he said, cutting her

off neatly and taking his seat behind his desk again. He didn't look up at her as he added, "The company jet will be at the airport. See that you're there, ready to go, by three o'clock."

Chapter 5

Kyra had one more meeting to handle before she could leave for home to get ready for this unexpected trip to Colorado. While her brain buzzed over the implications of just what this trip might mean, she told herself to let it go. To not think about it until she absolutely had to. Otherwise, she'd start gibbering to herself, and wouldn't that be a pretty picture?

Her assistant, Tracy, buzzed through. "Ms. Fortune, Mr. Hartsfield is here to see you."

Standing up, Kyra walked around her desk to greet the older man as he strode into her office.

George Hartsfield was at least eighty, but no one would know it from the way he moved. For a big man, he was light on his feet, and his sharp eyes never missed a trick. He wore a dark blue T-shirt over worn jeans held up by bright red suspenders. His work boots were scuffed and worn, and the overall impression he gave was that of a senior citizen down on his luck.

That impression couldn't have been more wrong.

As the head of the Hartsfield family, he ran an independent oil company that had been founded back in the days when Texas was a wide-open, wild-living place where fortunes were made and lost overnight. He'd staked his claims, drilled for oil and hit the big time, back when Kingston Fortune was just starting out.

"Ms. Fortune," George called out now, as if she were on the other side of the building. His booming voice matched his barrel chest, and his bald head gleamed in the overhead lights as he hurried toward Kyra, hand outstretched.

His massive hand swallowed hers in a firm grasp. "Good to see you again."

Kyra grinned up at him. She liked him. Had from the first. He was open, friendly and a living link to the days of Texas wildcatting. George himself would tell you he'd been around since the beginning of time. Self-educated, he liked to brag he'd never gotten past the eighth grade, and there wasn't a single thing about an oil field he didn't know.

"Mr. Hartsfield—"

"George," he said, releasing her hand and wagging an index finger at her.

"George," she repeated, smiling. "I'm hoping you've come here to tell me you've decided to join Voltage Energy."

Actually, she was more than hoping. She was praying. And counting on this deal being made. It would go a long way toward convincing the powers that be here at Voltage that she was too valuable an employee to lose.

George Hartsfield II was a fiercely independent man. More companies than Voltage had been trying for years to bring him and his fields into the fold. If Kyra could pull it off, she'd have the coup of the century.

He tucked one hand into his jeans pocket and jingled the coins and keys inside. "Truth to tell," he said, his voice nearly rattling the windows, "a few years ago, missy, I would've said no, flat out. And did. You're not the first to come sniffin' around my outfit. But I like to run my own show."

"That won't really change, George," Kyra said, feeling that lovely little glow sliding away from her even as she tried to grab it back. "You'll still make most of the decisions. Voltage only wants to help you expand. We can promise to increase your yield and—"

He held up one hand and shook his head. "Already heard the speech, little lady," he said, not unkindly. "And the thing of it is, I ain't as young as I used to be."

Kyra smiled and perched on the edge of her desk, enjoying this man immensely. Maybe it was still all right. Maybe he was going to sign up with Voltage and put the stamp of success on her career.

"I don't believe that for a minute," she said.

He wagged one finger at her again. "Don't kid a kidder, missy. Now, the reason I'm here is I've got one last question for you before I give you my decision. And I needed to see you in person to ask it. Phones are useless. Can't tell a thing about a man— or a woman," he corrected with a wink, "unless you can look 'em in the eye."

Just like that, the nerves were back, but she tamped them down and stood up to face him.

"Shoot," she said, wishing all of her clients were this forthright and easy to deal with.

"You're one of the Fortunes," he stated.

"Yes." Kyra flinched instinctively. She wasn't ashamed of her family name, but she'd never wanted to trade on it. And she didn't want to win the Hartsfield account because it, either. She wanted to win because she'd earned it. Because she was good at her job.

"Don't get your hump over the dashboard now," he soothed.

She blinked, then laughed. She couldn't help it. "My what?"

He chuckled and shook his head. "Old sayings from an old man, pay no never mind." He pulled his hand free of his pocket and scrubbed it across the gray whiskers stubbling his jaw. "My point is this. You being a Fortune don't hold much weight with me one way or the other. A name don't mean a damn thing unless the person carrying it is strong enough to make something of it."

He narrowed those sharp eyes on her speculatively. "I guess what I'm saying is, Kingston Fortune was a man to be reckoned with. Ryan Fortune is someone to trust. Someone strong enough to hold up the Fortune name. What I need to know is, are you?"

Kyra lifted her chin and met the big man's gaze squarely. "A fair question, George. I can tell you this. I came to work here instead of Fortune TX, Ltd., because I wanted to make my own way. Because I didn't want to cash in on the Fortune name." She took a step closer to the older man, who was watching her with an assessing eye. "But that doesn't mean I'm not proud of my name—or that I don't know what that name stands for. I am strong enough to carry it, George. I give you my word. As a Fortune. You can trust Voltage to be your partner, not a usurper."

He studied her for a full minute, then, apparently satisfied, offered her his hand again. When she shook it firmly, he said, "That's good enough for me, Kyra. I expect my lawyers will want things a little more formal—" he gave her a wink and a grin "—but where I come from, a handshake is enough to seal a deal."

Kyra smiled back and felt as though she'd just been awarded a medal. This was what she loved. This moment, when two people met and decided the future.

This man was trusting her to keep safe a company he'd spent a lifetime building. And it wasn't just because she'd been born into the Fortune family.

It was because she'd earned the right to be called a Fortune.

"If you'd like," Carol offered, "I'd be more than happy to accompany you on this trip."

"No, thanks." Garrett glanced at his assistant as she paused just inside the doorway to his office. He'd already dictated the last of the letters and memos he needed taken care of. And now all he wanted to do was straighten up his desk, go home and grab his bag. The sooner they got started on this trip, the sooner it would be over.

Damn it.

A trip with Kyra wasn't something he'd planned on. In fact, he'd spent the last couple of days trying to keep his distance from her. Cowardly, he knew. But he had little choice. Any kind of a relationship with the woman was out of the question. Yet, ever since that night at Rio's, he'd been spending far too much time thinking about her.

He couldn't seem to forget how she'd felt in his arms. The scent of her. The slow slide of her legs against his.

Which only went to prove that he'd been too long without a woman.

He'd let the company suck up his life.

But then, he had good reason for that, too, didn't he? He'd been engaged—twice. And each time, he'd discovered in the nick of time that he was sadly lacking when it came to being a good judge of character.

Since the last broken engagement, he'd turned his back on any kind of a relationship. He'd refused to trust his own instincts again. Refused to set himself up for another fall. If his life was a little barren at the moment, at least he wasn't being lied to by a woman who wanted nothing more from him but his bank account.

But Kyra could be different, his brain kept taunting him. She was a Fortune, after all. She didn't have to marry for money. Didn't have to lie and cheat her way into a relationship.

The very fact that he was seriously considering becoming involved with a woman who made him crazy showed just how bad a shape he was in.

Shaking his head, he closed a file folder and set it to one side of his desk. Only then did he notice that Carol was still there. In the doorway. Watching him.

Impatience stirred within.

Damn it, this was all Kyra's fault, too. He'd been perfectly happy with his administrative assistant. Carol had been nothing but exceptionally efficient for years. Until Kyra, he hadn't been willing to see that he'd turned over too much of his life into Carol's competent hands.

But that wasn't his admin's fault. "What is it, Carol?"

"Nothing really," she said, taking a step or two toward him. Her dark curly hair was caught at the back of her head with a silver barrette and her dark green business suit was, of course, impeccable. Folding her hands together at her waist, she said, "It's just that I don't believe Ms. Fortune is the proper person to accompany you to this meeting."

Curiosity warred now with the impatience nibbling at him. "And why's that?"

She smiled sweetly. "Really, Mr. Wolff. She's a

nice enough young woman, but as a member of the Fortune family, she's hardly the right person to represent the best interests of Voltage."

Garrett pushed away from his desk and stood up, riding a suddenly fierce wave of both outrage and a weird sense of protectiveness. He really didn't want to explore the reasons behind his unexpected urge to defend Kyra Fortune, so he shoved that thought to the back of his mind.

Buttoning his suit jacket with one hand, he reached for his oxblood leather briefcase with the other. Then, meeting Carol's wide-eyed stare, he said, "The senior partners have assigned Ms. Fortune to this meeting. I should think that they are in a better position than you to understand what is in this company's best interests."

"Of course." She went stiff as a board, and her eyes flickered with something that might have been insult or injury.

He wasn't sure which, and at the moment he didn't really care.

Heading around his desk, he stalked past her to the door. Over his shoulder, he said abruptly, "I should be back in two days."

When he was gone, Carol didn't move. Standing in the middle of Garrett Wolff's office, she clutched the hurt to her like a worn, tattered blanket.

And she heaped silent curses on Kyra Fortune's head.

* * *

Kyra was racing around her condo like a crazy person.

She'd already arranged for her neighbor to take care of her cat, Viggo, who was named after one of the sexiest movie stars she'd ever seen. She'd arranged to have her mail held at the post office. Her plants could probably use a few days off from her incessant overwatering, so she wouldn't worry about them. And everything else in the tiny efficiency condo would be just fine without her.

A sobering thought, she realized as she walked across her tidy, almost unlived-in living room. She'd focused so much on building her career over the last several years, she'd forgotten all about building a life.

Oh, she dated, sporadically, though heaven knew her last date had been so long ago, she couldn't even remember who the guy was, let alone when it was. Kyra scooped her hair back from her face and shook her head. A sad state of things, no doubt. But she'd made her decision years ago. To not get involved. To not search for love.

The only reason a woman looked for love was to eventually get married and have children. And that was not in Kyra's game plan. She'd seen up close and personal just what kind of prison marriage could be for a woman. No way was she interested in purposely stepping into a cage.

But it wasn't just dating that had suffered along the way. She'd lost track of most of her friends, since they didn't have a lot of patience for Kyra's habit of breaking engagements or postponing plans. The only close friend she'd been able to keep over the years was Isa. And that was only because Isabella Sanchez refused to cut her loose. Thank heaven.

Heading into the kitchen, Kyra opened the fridge, pulled out a jug of iced tea and poured herself a tall glass. Taking a sip, she looked around the room and realized that but for the calendar tacked to the refrigerator with silly flower-shaped magnets, the kitchen was devoid of the slightest personal stamp. It could have been an empty room in a model house.

And that theme stretched through the rest of the condo, too. She'd had some ideas for decorating when she'd bought the place, but they'd gone by the wayside, buried under her determination to build a name for herself at Voltage.

The walls were still beige, the carpet was still boring and the curtains were the same ones that had been hanging there when she'd bought the unit four years ago.

"Not exactly a nester, are you, Kyra?" she murmured. Once upon a time, she recalled, leaning back against the tiled counter, she'd had other plans. Plans to buy an old house and restore it. Plans to paint each room in her house a different, vibrant color. To fill her world with all of the bright, silly "fripperies" that her father had never allowed in the home where she'd grown up.

Her hand clenched tightly around the icy-cold glass as memories flooded her mind. As if it were yesterday, she could see the empty barrenness of her childhood home. She saw her mother slipping through the house like a ghost, afraid to be noticed, afraid to catch her husband's attention.

And she saw her older brother, Vincent, always tall and strong, standing between Kyra and the fury of her father's embittered rage. Leonard Fortune had never been the man he'd always imagined himself to be, and that failure had colored everything in his life. He'd made his wife miserable, his children terrified and himself unbearable.

But all those years under Leonard Fortune's thumb had forged steel in his children. God knew, he hadn't meant to do them any favors. If anything, he'd done his best to break them all.

Except for her.

Guilt pinged around inside her like an old familiar ache. She'd never had to suffer the same kind of abuse her siblings had, because Vincent, her oldest brother, had protected her from it. He'd given up a lot to keep her safe. To keep her from buckling beneath their father's self-hatred.

She owed Vincent more than she could ever repay.

So, if she had to live in an impersonal little condo, she would. If she had to work twenty hour days, she would.

And if she had to travel to Colorado with the devil himself, she damn well *would*.

Carrying her tea back to the bedroom, she set it down on the pine bedside table and turned back to her packing.

When the phone rang a few minutes later, Kyra snatched it up, tucked it between her chin and shoulder and kept packing. "Hello?"

"Hi, Kyra, it's me."

Smiling, she dropped her royal-blue sweater on top of the packed clothes in her suitcase, then turned and plopped down onto the side of her bed. "Hi, Susan," she said, picturing her sister sitting at her cozy kitchen table with a cup of steaming herbal tea in front of her. "What's up?"

There was a long pause, and a flash of worry darted through Kyra. "What is it? What's wrong? Are you okay?"

"I'm fine."

"Ethan?" Kyra prodded, instinctively responding to the heaviness in her sister's voice.

"He's fine, too," Susan assured her, and Kyra relaxed a little when she heard the smile in her sister's voice. It happened every time the woman spoke about her new husband.

Pulling her legs up, Kyra folded them beneath her, cross-legged and stared across the room at the open window and the trees beyond. As always, the sight of the wind sighing through the new green leaves calmed her.

"Tell me," she said softly.

"It's Ryan," Susan said. "He doesn't have much longer."

"Oh, God." Kyra squeezed her eyes shut and took the blow. She'd known for a month or more that Ryan Fortune was dying, but somehow, Kyra had convinced herself that he would find a way to beat the death sentence handed him. If anyone could have, it would have been him. "How long?"

"No one knows for sure," Susan said with a sigh. "But my guess is a few days at most."

"I'm so sorry," she said softly, knowing it wasn't enough. Could never be enough.

"I know. Me, too. It's just so sad at the ranch right now, Kyra." She paused, then continued. "Ryan's kids are coming in, gathering. There are telegrams and flowers arriving every minute, it seems. And just yesterday, two ambassadors and a prince showed up at the Double Crown just to say goodbye to him."

In spite of the sorrow welling within, Kyra

smiled. "Not surprising, is it? Ryan's touched more people's lives than anyone I've ever known. He's always seemed larger than life. Hard to believe he's going to die."

"Lily's not having much luck accepting that." Tears clogged Susan's voice, but she choked them back. "I swear, she's holding on by the skin of her teeth."

"This must be killing her."

"By inches."

Kyra rubbed her temples, massaging a small headache trying to settle in. "Is there anything I can do?"

"Honestly? No." Susan blew out a breath and said, "I just wanted you to know. To be prepared."

How did you prepare for something like this? Ryan Fortune, an admirable man to the rest of the world, had always seemed like the kingpin of the Fortune family to Kyra. He was a presence. Not only to the family, but to Texas. The whole world was going to seem just a little bit smaller without him. And when he was really gone, she wondered, without his kindness, his leadership to lean on, what would the rest of them do?

"Hey," her sister asked, "you okay?"

"Not especially," Kyra answered, then squared her shoulders, as she knew Ryan would expect them all to do. "But I will be."

"It's not going to be easy on any of us, Kyra. But we'll all get through it."

"I know. Look, do you need anything? I mean, I'm guessing you're staying close to the Double Crown, helping out."

Susan sighed into the phone. "Yeah, I've pretty much been camping out in the cottage I used to rent. Ethan's been a sweetheart about this, too."

"He's a good guy, Susan. He understands what family means."

"Yeah. Guess he does at that. And God knows Ryan means as much to him as to any of us."

Kyra reached for the dark blue sweater, dragged it across her lap and idly started folding it again as she said, "I'm supposed to fly out to Colorado this afternoon. Some business meeting for Voltage. I can try to get out of it."

"Don't. Go to your meeting. And don't feel bad about leaving town, honey. There's nothing anyone can do, and to be honest, there're so many people here now, I wish I could get rid of some of them. But Lily says that Ryan is enjoying seeing everyone."

"Okay, then. I'll only be gone a couple of days, though. So I'll come right over as soon as I get home." It didn't seem right, leaving just when her family was suffering a crisis. "How's Lily holding up?"

"About how you'd expect." Speaking to someone

else, Susan said, "Yes, I'll be right there. Hey, Kyra, gotta go. I'll keep you posted."

Kyra held on to the phone long after her sister had hung up, as if needing even that tenuous connection with her family. She should be staying here, in Red Rock. She should be out at the ranch with the rest of the family. Helping. Praying. Doing *something*.

But maybe, she thought, as she set the phone down and scooted off the four-poster bed, going on this trip was exactly what Ryan would expect. He'd always kept his promises. He'd managed to have both a family and a career. And what better way could she show her appreciation for all he'd been than to carry on just as he'd always done?

Grimly, she shoved the rest of her things into the black leather bag and zipped it closed. Then she dragged it off the bed and wheeled it to the front door.

Grabbing up her purse, she headed out to keep her appointment with Garrett Wolff.

Because Fortunes never quit.

Chapter 6

"If you have to fly, this is really the only way to do it." Kyra sat back in the plush cream-colored leather seat, planted the toe of one stylish pump against the thick carpet and gave her chair a little swivel.

Garrett stared at her from across the plane. "You don't like flying, I take it?"

"Not particularly," she admitted, and silently called herself a whopping great liar. She *hated* flying. Absolutely loathed it, with a bone-deep fear that started as she boarded a jet, and didn't let loose until she'd landed again and was in a taxi headed away from the airport.

It just wasn't natural, she always told herself.

Something as heavy as a jet should *not* be able to stay up in the air. Gravity, after all, was a pretty convincing fact of science. What went up always came down. And not necessarily when planned.

But she'd never been one to give in to her fears. So she stepped onto planes regularly and then held her breath until she was safely back on the ground where she belonged.

One corner of Garrett's mouth lifted. "Didn't notice any loud praying or chanting."

She smiled briefly. "Hey, I'm no hypocrite. I figure since I don't spend much time praying ordinarily, God wouldn't like it much if I jumped down his throat just because I'm on a plane."

"You think the Almighty is paying that close attention?"

"If he is, I sure don't want to be in a plane when I offend him."

"Good point," Garrett acknowledged. Then he asked, "So why don't you like flying? It's safer than—"

"Driving on the highways," she finished for him in a rote, singsong voice. "Yes, I've heard those statistics. But the thing is, if you fall out of a car, it's a much shorter drop."

"So it's the altitude that bothers you."

"A big part of it, sure," she acknowledged, and resolutely kept her gaze from straying to one of the

windows. On a commercial flight she always reserved an aisle seat. She claimed, to anyone who
asked, that she liked the extra room for her long
legs and that she didn't want to have to climb over
anyone if she needed to make a restroom run. But
the simple truth was she didn't want to be able to
look out a window.

Bad enough to know you're thirty thousand feet
up. No reason to have to look down, too.

Garrett was still gazing at her, waiting for her
to finish, so she added, "I don't like the idea of not
being in control."

"There's a surprise."

One blond eyebrow winged up and Kyra tilted
her head to examine him more closely. "Was that
humor?"

He took a sip of coffee and looked from her to the
file opened across his lap and back again. "Probably
not."

"No," she said, feeling a little of the airborne tension draining away. "I suppose not."

Interesting. A flash of warmth in a man she'd
always thought to be stone cold. But then, she'd
sensed plenty of warmth that night at Rio's, hadn't
she? Warmth and interest and—

Kyra shifted uneasily in her seat, then tensed
slightly as the plane hit a patch of turbulence. A
lesser plane would have shuddered and groaned

through the pocket of rough air. But not this elegant piece of machinery. It only shivered daintily, whispered of "Oops, was that trouble?" then flew on, undisturbed.

Kyra, though, felt every quiver. Her fingers curled over the end of the armrests and her stomach did a sharp dive that left her mouth dry and her nerves tingling. Her gaze shot up and down the plane, as if waiting to see chairs toppled or pillows suddenly tossed to the floor.

"It's nothing," he said.

Kyra shot him a quick glance and swallowed hard. She really hated having him see her go all weenie. "Yeah. I know that. I just don't *know* that, you know?"

A short, sharp laugh shot from his throat. "Oh, perfectly clear."

Her heartbeat thundered wildly in her chest and her throat remained as dry as East Texas while she waited for the turbulence to pass. Her grip on the armrests had her knuckles whitening even as the muscles in her arms strained and complained.

Finally, everything seemed to smooth out again, and she fought her fears until they were nothing but a tiny ball of dread in the bottom of her stomach.

"So," Kyra said, keeping her voice as light as she could manage in an attempt to reclaim her reputation as a cool customer, "since you know now that I hate flying, how about some conversation?"

Anything to keep her mind off being this high in the air without so much as a parachute. And besides, if left to her own devices, her brain would only slide evilly between terror and the misery of knowing that even as she sat here, Ryan Fortune was dying.

Garrett lifted his gaze from the file that had been absorbing most of his attention since they'd left Red Rock more than an hour ago. "Sure you don't want to rethink your stance on prayer?"

"There's that surprising little show of humor again. Seriously, Mr. Wolff, if I didn't know better, I'd think you were almost human." As soon as the words were out, she groaned and winced. For heaven's sake, the man was not only her boss, but he already didn't like her. Was there any reason to antagonize him even further? "Sorry. Flying makes me nervous. Nervous makes me talk. Not always a good combination."

Closing the file, Garrett laid it across his lap and looked at her. "If being out of control bothers you so much, why not take flying lessons?"

"Good idea in theory," she said, then waved one hand to encompass the plane and the open sky. "Only problem with that is, to take flying lessons, I'd have to actually, you know, fly."

"Ah." His mouth curved briefly.

"I thought about it once," she said, grabbing hold of the conversation and giving it a hard shake. "But then the pilot wanted to take me up in one of those little rubber-band planes."

"A Cessna?"

"Whatever." She shook her head at the memory. The thing had looked like a toy. And its propeller had not been big enough to convince Kyra it would be able to stay in the air. What if it stopped? What if it broke? "The guy said it was a great little plane. He'd been flying it for thirty years with no problem. You know what that told me?"

"I'm fascinated," Garrett said with a shake of his own head. "What did that tell you? That the man was experienced? The plane dependable?"

"Nope. It told me the plane was old and so was the pilot."

He laughed, and despite her nerves, Kyra felt the hard jolt of surprise and interest poke at her insides. The man was gorgeous when he smiled. A grin did amazing things for his eyes. And that laugh reverberated throughout her body, acting on her nerves like a tuning fork. Plus, he looked…really *hot*.

"Experience doesn't count for anything with you?" he asked, still chuckling.

Kyra went with it, determined now to see that full-wattage smile again. "Hey, I like old doctors. That kind of experience is handy. But old pilots? No, thanks. Do I really want to be alone in the plane with him if his heart stops?" She paused, thought about that and asked, "How old is our pilot, by the way?"

"Forties."

"Oh. That's probably okay, then."

"I'm sure he'll be happy to hear that," Garrett said. "So the old saying about how you're safe unless it's your time to go doesn't mean anything to you?"

Kyra released her stranglehold on the armrests and leaned forward in her seat. "That's fine and dandy, unless it's your *pilot's* time to go."

Garrett looked at her in stunned surprise for a long minute, then grinned again. "You're a fascinating woman, Kyra Fortune."

Oh boy, that grin of his was really powerful. It punched at her unexpectedly and rocked her right down to her toes. But maybe it wasn't as sexually charged as she thought. Maybe it was due to her stark terror at being in the air, for heaven's sake, combined with her long bout of celibacy and solitude.

If so, she'd better get a grip on her nerves and make a date the minute they got back home.

Oh yeah. Fantasizing about the boss? Not a good career move in anybody's book.

"Thanks," she said finally. "I try." Then, because she was still nervous and her mouth was pretty much running wild here anyway, she added, "And that smile of yours is a heck of a weapon."

He blinked at her.

"Right. Never mind. Shouldn't have said that," she muttered, and gave in to a sudden, restless urge to move around. Actually, to run away from what she'd just said. Unfortunately, that was another downside to plane travel. There was nowhere to run when you needed to. "Sorry. It's just… You smiled and I thought, wow. It surprised me. I shouldn't have said it out loud, though, but to be fair, I warned you about the whole nerves thing."

"Yes, you did."

He watched her as she unsnapped her seat belt and pushed herself to her feet. She felt his gaze on her, hot and steady, and her stomach swirled.

Oh, boy.

The same nerves that had prompted her mouth to charge ahead at full steam were now pushing her to move. Sitting still only seemed to make her more nervous, which would mean more talking, which could hardly be considered a good thing.

Especially now.

She walked up and down the wide aisle, with long, sure steps. More like a forced march than a stroll. She trailed her fingertips across the high backs of the leather seats she passed, hoping for a nonchalant sort of feel. It didn't work, since she could still detect Garrett's gaze boring into her back with every step. She wished she knew what he was thinking, but at the same time, she thought maybe it was just as well she didn't know.

She couldn't believe she'd told him he was gorgeous. Or that he had a killer smile. Heck, she couldn't believe she was here, trapped in a plane with a man who only the week before she'd considered public enemy number one. And now...she didn't.

At the rear of the plane, she knew, there was a completely outfitted bedroom, for those long, uncomfortable flights when one of the Voltage execs would need to catch up on his sleep. She'd peeked in before, and though it wasn't as plush as the bedroom on the Fortune family private jet, it was pretty nice.

Of course, at the moment, with just her and Garrett Wolff as passengers, Kyra turned her mind away from all thoughts of that bedroom. It was safer that way. Instead, she did an about-face and walked back toward him, still talking.

"It's a nice jet." Not as nice as Ryan Fortune's, she added silently, but still pretty impressive. At the thought of Ryan, regret whispered through her again. She should be at home with the family. She should have told Garrett she couldn't make the trip.

But she couldn't really afford to make anyone at Voltage mad at the moment, either, could she?

"Why don't you sit down?" Garrett asked suddenly.

"Nerves," she muttered helplessly.

"I thought you said nerves made you talk too much."

"Yes," she agreed, "but walking, talking, they sort of go together and—"

The plane dipped unexpectedly, shifting to the left, and Kyra felt her balance dissolve in a heartbeat. With a whoop, she tumbled over onto Garrett's lap. Instantly, his arms came around her, holding tight as the plane plummeted a few thousand feet in what seemed like seconds.

"I knew it! I knew planes were bad!" She clutched at his shoulders and whipped her head from side to side as if she would actually be able to see danger and react to it.

She didn't care that she was on his lap, crushing the file folder beneath her. Didn't care that it probably wasn't appropriate to be grabbing hold of her boss, or to have his arms wrapped around her. She only wanted something, someone, to hold on to.

As quickly as it had started, the turbulence ended and the plane straightened out and stopped descending. A fact for which Kyra was immeasurably grateful.

"It's probably nothing," Garrett said, but he didn't release her. With his right arm wrapped firmly around her middle, he held her on his lap while he reached for the intercom button with his left hand.

"Captain Harris?"

"Yes. Sorry about that, Mr. Wolff."

The pilot's voice sounded tinny, but calm. "Hit a wall of rough there, but we're okay now. ETA in Colorado, forty-five minutes. Weather services claim a storm's blowing in, though. Should hit the Denver area sometime tonight."

"Thanks." Garrett leaned back in his seat and looked up at Kyra. "You okay?"

"A storm? What kind of storm? Rain. Probably rain."

"Probably. So are you all right?"

"Yeah." She pulled in a deep breath and forced a smile that felt as though it would crack her face. "I'm fine, just—"

"Nervous," he finished for her.

His arm was still wrapped around her, and Kyra felt the warm, solid strength of him surrounding her. The nerves clawing at her stomach eased—only to be replaced by a whole new set of nerves.

And these had nothing to do with flying.

Nope. These were connected to the fact that she was sitting on Garrett Wolff's lap and, if she wasn't mistaken, he was enjoying the situation.

A curl of something warm and wicked spun through her, and Kyra tried to focus on breathing.

But it wasn't easy. Not with his face so close, his eyes locked onto hers and his mouth just a kiss away.

Seconds ticked past lazily. The drone of the engines became more of a purr. Heat poured from Garrett into Kyra, and she felt herself slowly, slowly dissolving.

His gorgeous eyes glittered with a hunger that matched what she felt roaring within her. Her hands tightened on his shoulders. His arm around her waist tugged her in closer.

She felt his breath on her face.

Her stomach did a slow slide to her toes, while her heartbeat jumped.

She leaned closer.

Closer.

"Mr. Wolff?"

"Geez!" Kyra jumped in his arms, just missing smashing his nose with her forehead.

The female voice spilled through the intercom and shattered whatever spell had held them in place. Kyra felt disoriented. Garrett looked furious.

Instantly, Kyra bolted, pushing out of his arms and standing on legs none too steady. Her body whimpered, but her brain shut down the longing. She told herself that she hadn't actually felt Garrett's body harden beneath hers. She hadn't actually been fantasizing about kissing him.

She scrubbed both hands across her face and sat

down on the opposite side of the plane. Quickly she buckled her seat belt and sternly told herself to stay put. To keep her distance. To, for heaven's sake, never fall into the man's lap again.

"Mr. Wolff?"

The voice came again, a little louder this time, and Kyra realized he hadn't answered the summons yet. She glanced at him and found him staring at her through blue eyes that looked as stormy as the sea. His expression was unreadable, and Kyra wished she knew what he was thinking, what he was feeling.

Was it only she who'd felt that momentary blast of heat? That incredible urge to—

Garrett leaned over, pressed the intercom button once more and practically snarled, "Yes?"

"I'm sorry, sir." The female flight attendant's voice was frosty. "I don't mean to interrupt, but I wondered if you and Ms. Fortune would care for some more coffee or tea."

He looked at her, a question in his eyes.

Kyra nodded. Good. A distraction was good. "Coffee. Thanks."

He hit the button again. "Two more coffees. Thank you."

When the intercom was quiet again, Garrett deliberately kept his gaze from meeting Kyra's. He picked up the file folder he'd been reading earlier, smoothed out the wrinkles made by her butt landing on his lap, and studied it like a man reading a map in the desert, desperately looking for the last water hole.

He couldn't have made his position any clearer, she thought with a pang of something that was not disappointment. Clearly, he wasn't going to acknowledge that moment of insanity. He was going to pretend that nothing had happened between them in that one little slice of time.

Well, fine. Better this way, anyway, she thought. At least she knew where they stood. Back on the shaky ground of being enemies.

And before she gave in to the urge to walk and talk off her nervousness again, she'd nail her feet to the floor and sew her lips shut.

Chapter 7

"We should have stayed at the airport." Kyra's voice was quiet, tinged with just a hint of fear.

He couldn't blame her. Just outside Denver, the promised storm had hit. At first, there hadn't been more than a few snow flurries gusting past the car. Now, though, things were different.

Garrett's hands fisted on the steering wheel, his knuckles whitening. Since getting off the plane, they'd hardly spoken two words to each other. Which was probably just as well, he conceded.

It was better all the way around that they keep a safe distance between them—even if it was only emotional. Sure, they were stuck with each other's company for a couple of days, but nothing said they had to talk.

Besides, talking wasn't what he wanted from her.

In a flash, his brain tripped back to that moment in the plane when the turbulence had dropped Kyra into his lap. His body had reacted so quickly, so fiercely, it had taken his breath away. With his arms around her, her hands on his shoulders, her mouth just a breath away from his, Garrett had damn near given in to the instinctive urge to kiss her.

Taste her.

If it hadn't been for the flight attendant interrupting them… He'd never been both grateful and annoyed at the same time before. By the time Kyra had lurched off his lap, he'd been forced to keep that stupid file folder open across his legs just to keep her from seeing what her nearness had done to him.

"Hello?" Kyra said, her voice sharp, worried. "Are you in a coma or something?"

"Wide awake," he snarled. "And concentrating."

Kyra peered through the windshield at the swirling wall of white just beyond. "I can't believe it's snowing this hard in April."

"Not too unusual for Colorado," Garrett muttered, and kept his gaze fixed determinedly on the road in front of them. Not that it was helping much. In the last fifteen minutes, the snow flurries had thickened until it felt as though he was driving through a snow globe shaken by an angry child.

On either side of the two-lane highway, tall pines dipped and swayed in the rush of wind and snow. The headlights only served to illuminate the gusts of white, leaving the road pretty much to guesswork. He'd been reduced to hugging the right side of the road, following the curve of the trees. The double yellow line was gone, swallowed by the snow. Why they'd had to meet at a private estate rather than at the airport hotel, he didn't know.

"Remind me to stay in Texas from now on," Kyra whispered.

"I'm with you on that one," Garrett muttered, thinking about Red Rock, wishing they were both back there now, with the sun blasting out of a brassy sky. Not to mention Kyra locked away in her office and he in his own.

"Maybe we should go back."

He glanced at her. "There's nowhere to turn around, Kyra. We keep going."

"Right. But will we even *see* the turnoff?"

"Hell if I know."

"Not real comforting."

"You want comfort?" he asked. "At least we're on the ground."

"Right. Good. Car better than plane." She forced a smile. He could see the tension in her eyes and knew what that brief smile had cost her. She had spine. More strength than he'd ever thought.

Flying made her crazy, but she didn't let her fears keep her out of the sky. She could talk a man into the ground when nerves had her, but she wasn't afraid to tell you what she was thinking.

"We should probably stop until this snow quits," she murmured, "don't you think?"

"Stop where?"

"Good point." She wiped her palm across the passenger-side window, as if it would clear her view. "It's getting thicker."

"Yeah," he said, squinting past the wiper blades that whipped ferociously across the windshield. "I know."

This stretch of highway was almost deserted. He'd seen only two other cars in the last hour, and the only house they'd passed had been more than a mile back.

"Do you have any idea at all where we are?" she asked.

He spared her a quick look and a shrug. "I'm not even sure we're on the right road anymore." It cost him to admit that, since like every other male in the world, he never liked to acknowledge that he might be lost. But in this blinding snow, it was impossible to know if he'd stayed on the main route or somehow taken a side road that would land them in the middle of nowhere.

The headlight beams bounced off the rushing snow and flashed right back at them. The wipers slapped the glass, but couldn't quite keep up with the thickening storm. Between gusts of wind the heater sighed, spewing warm air at the front seat, and still Garrett felt a chill right down to his bones.

Unless they got off this road and found shelter, they were an accident waiting to happen.

"What's that?"

Garrett glanced at her again. "What's what?"

"That. Don't you hear it?"

From a distance came what sounded like a fog-horn. Long, low, moaning, it cut through the wind, the snow, the cold, and made Garrett shiver with foreboding.

In the next instant, headlights speared through the windshield, brakes screamed, tires slid on ice and Kyra shrieked, "Look out!"

Garrett cursed, low and harsh, and then yanked the steering wheel to the right. As they crashed through trees and down a ravine into a snow-filled cavern of shadows, she heard the eighteen-wheeler zoom past them into the night.

"Kyra! You all right?"

She woke up to a white, silent world and a headache the size of West Texas. The deployed airbag was already deflating as she turned to look at Garrett in the darkness. "Yeah," she said. "I think so."

She lifted one hand to her forehead, half expecting to find her head sitting at an inhuman angle to her neck. Nope. Still there. Just aching like a bad tooth.

"Kyra?"

She blinked, focused, then nodded. "Right. I'm fine. You?"

"Yeah." He unsnapped his seat belt, then leaned over and did the same for her. "I'm fine. But the car's trashed. No way are we getting it back to the highway."

Back to the highway? Oh yeah. They'd been run off the road and were now sitting at the bottom of a ditch, snow-laden pine trees the only witnesses. "Great. Now what?"

"We've got to get out of here."

"And go where?" she asked, sliding her gaze from Garrett to the wall of white just outside the car.

"We passed a cabin about a mile down the road," he said, reaching into the back seat to drag out the coats they'd brought along. Pushing hers toward her, he shoved his arms through the sleeves of his own and then shifted in his seat to button it up. "Get your coat on, Kyra. We can't stay here."

She knew that. They'd freeze to death if they

stayed in the car. But the thought of walking a mile through the blowing snow filled her with dread. She looked out the window again and shivered.

"It'll be okay," he said, as if reading her mind. His voice was low, intimate and just a little impatient.

She turned her head to look at him and found his face only an inch or so from hers. Forcing a smile, she said, "I'm not much of a hiker."

"We'll make it."

She nodded because she knew they had no choice. But she really wished she were wearing hiking boots and thermal underwear instead of black slacks and trendy pumps. "Okay, then, let's go."

He opened his car door and instantly icy wind and a blast of snow rushed inside. Kyra dragged her coat on, grabbed her purse and opened her own door before she could chicken out. The teeth of the wind snapped at her, sending cold shards deep into her bones. She used numb fingers to fumble her coat buttons closed, and wished briefly that she'd gone more for warmth than style when she'd bought it. But at home she was only in the cold long enough to run from her condo to her car.

Here, it was different.

Here, it was freezing.

Garrett came around the end of the car, grabbed her elbow and steered her back up the ravine to the highway, where walking would be easier. Her elegant black pumps slipped and slid on the snowy ground, and her bare ankles soon felt like blocks of ice.

"Have to keep moving," Garrett shouted, close to her ear. While they walked, he dug out his cell phone, stabbed at the numbers then cursed. "No service. Keep walking."

She knew that, but it didn't make it easy. One foot in front of the other. Fall, sprawl in the snow, get up and do it again. Slowly, determinedly, she kept pace with him, but was grateful for his firm grip on her arm.

Up on the highway, the wind had free rein. There were no trees to block it. Nothing to ease the bite of it. She dipped her head and plowed along in Garrett's wake. Alongside them, the pine trees bent and swayed in the wind, as if dancing to music only they could hear. Her teeth chattered and each breath felt as if splinters of ice were scraping her lungs.

Snow dusted them until they looked as if they'd been tarred and feathered. Flakes slipped under their coats, slid beneath the collars of their shirts and snaked along their spines, driving the cold deeper. Their footprints were filled in as soon as they'd moved on.

And the snow kept falling.

The wind kept howling.

Kyra lost track of time. Lost track of everything

but the need to focus on moving first one foot, then the other. Her brain raced while her body plodded.

She thought of roaring fires, blistering sunlight and snuggling up to a warm body beneath a down quilt. She thought of summer days and long, hot nights. She thought about burrowing into Garrett's chest and feeling his arms come around her.

Her steps slowed as her body grew tired.

"Keep moving, Kyra."

"I am." Too weary to shout, she let her anger out in a snarl.

"Not fast enough. You're slowing down."

"Cold. Too cold," she murmured, and hated that she sounded whiny. But she felt whiny. Every inch of her body ached with fatigue and cold. She wasn't dressed for this. And working out three days a week in a climate-controlled gym just didn't prepare a person for hiking through snow wearing now-ruined pumps.

"Gonna quit on me, Fortune?" he asked, dipping his head so that his words came hot and furious beside her ear.

"Didn't say that," she snapped, feeling a small spark of irritation burst into life in the pit of her stomach. She straightened, clenched her teeth and muttered, "I can make it."

"I don't know," he goaded. "You're looking a little wiped."

That tiny spark of irritation blossomed and grew, warming her a little with the flames of righteous indignation. "Don't you worry about me," she said, grinding out each word. "I can make it if you can."

"Bet you can't."

She flashed him a glare. "How much?"

"Fifty bucks says you fold before we get to that cabin."

"You're on," she said quickly, reacting to the challenge just as she always did. Don't think about it, just take it, then do whatever you had to do to win.

She'd always been competitive. It came from being the youngest of four children. Always jockeying for position. Always having to shout just to make sure people knew you were there. Always trying to be noticed. To be better. To be someone.

This is not the time for self-psychoanalysis, Kyra.

Instead, she gave in to the urge to win. To compete. She would use whatever tools she had to help her make this trek.

Pulling her arm free of his grasp, she said, "And if I have to drag you the last half mile or so, I want a hundred."

"Deal," he said, and grabbed her arm again.

She would have fought him on it, feeling the need to stand on her own two feet. But the simple truth was she needed the stability his strength offered. Her feet kept sliding on the snow-covered road, and if she fell down one more time, she wasn't at all sure she'd be able to get back up again, bet or no bet.

"The Fortunes are supposed to be tough," he said, and she heard laughter in his tone.

"Tougher than you can imagine," she replied, her breath huffing out in a white cloud in front of her face.

He had no idea, she told herself. No idea at all what it was like to grow up as the child of Leonard Fortune. Maybe her crowd of cousins had grown up at ease with the world, but *her* father's children had had to fight for everything they'd ever had.

"Prove it," he taunted. "Keep moving, Kyra. Just keep moving."

"I *am* moving," she said, planting one foot in front of the other, wincing as daggerlike jabs of cold stabbed her legs with every step.

"Not much farther."

"You've been saying that for hours."

"Not hours."

"Feels like it."

"I know. Almost there."

Kyra's body was on autopilot, but her brain kept ticking. She knew what Garrett was doing. By making her mad, by forcing her to concentrate on proving him wrong, he was giving her the strength to make this hike through what felt like the back forty of the North Pole.

He was every bit as cold as she, and just as unprepared to face a howling winter storm. Yet he had the strength to push on. The determination to make sure *she* kept moving. Admiration welled up inside her.

She'd always thought of him as a brilliant businessman. But she'd had no idea that beneath those elegantly cut suits beat the heart of an adventurer.

And oh, she was grateful for it.

"There it is," he called out.

Thank God.

She squinted through the wind-driven snow and spotted a shadow among the trees. About a hundred yards off the highway, the cabin sat squat and dark. But to Kyra, it looked at the moment like a five-star hotel.

The snow was nearly knee-high now, and walking was harder than ever. Especially as they struggled uphill toward the cabin.

Still Garrett kept moving, kept his grip firm and strong on her arm and didn't let her slow. Kyra reached deep inside for the last of her strength and drew on it to help her march at his side.

"Come on, Kyra. Almost there."

His words washed over her, promising rest, warmth. And she knew in that moment that she would have followed him anywhere.

When they finally reached the postage-stamp-size front porch, Garrett pounded on the door while Kyra leaned heavily against the wall. The rough logs bit into her back, but she barely felt them. It was as though her whole body had been shot through with Novocain.

No lights shone through the snow-frosted glass and no sound came from within. There was no answer to Garrett's pounding on the door as they stood huddled together, while snow and wind surrounded them with icy arms.

He tried the knob. It turned, and Garrett opened the door to a cold, dark room that looked like a little slice of heaven to Kyra. Pulling her in after him, he closed the door, and instantly the howling wind was reduced to a whine.

Shivering, she wrapped her arms around her middle and focused on standing upright.

Garrett hit a light switch and, when nothing happened, said, "Power must be out."

She almost laughed. "Of course."

"Come on, sit down." He drew her to a sofa and pushed her onto it, then went around the room, feeling his way in the dark.

Finally, she heard the scratch of a match, and a tiny flame erupted, blazing in the shadows like a bonfire.

"No power, but there're plenty of candles." In a

couple of seconds, he had five of them lit, staggering across the fireplace mantel in a jagged line of light.

"Whoever lives here left the fire ready to start. You'll be warm in a few minutes."

"Good," she said, despite her chattering teeth. She felt cold right down to her bones and promised herself she'd never curse a hot Texas summer again. "That'd be really good."

She closed her eyes and leaned back on the over-stuffed cushions. Nothing had ever felt quite so wonderful. She was still freezing, still felt the cold like knives stabbing at her legs. But she was out of the wind, out of the snow.

That was a start.

From behind her closed lids, she saw light flicker, and she learned the comforting crackle of flames.

She felt herself dissolving into the old sofa and knew she didn't have the energy to move again. She'd just sit right here, she thought. Until spring thaw. But wasn't it already spring?

Supposed to be, she thought, frowning as her muscles went lax and limp.

"No you don't," Garrett said. "No going to sleep until you're defrosted."

He grabbed her hands and pulled her from the couch, despite her efforts at shoving him away.

"Tired," she murmured. "Leave me alone."

"Not yet," he said, and before she could protest

again, he swung her up in his arms and carried her closer to the flames leaping in the hearth.

"Put me down, damn it," she whispered, and hardly noticed that her orders weren't carrying a lot of weight.

"I am," he said, sinking down on his knees on a thick, braided rug. "Right here."

"Damn it, Garrett, back off," she said, even as the heat reached out for her. Instinctively, she turned toward the flames. Pins and needles prickled along her skin as her body temperature slowly started to rise.

"You're freezing, Kyra," Garrett stated flatly. "We've got to get you warm again."

She paid no attention to him. She was much too busy trying to soak in as much heat as she could. She welcomed the uncomfortable stinging on her skin because she knew it meant she was thawing out.

Garrett, meanwhile, stripped off his own coat, then went to work on her. "What're you doing?" she yelped, and tried to fend off his hands.

"I'm getting you out of those wet clothes."

"Like hell!" She scooted backward, slapping at his hands, pushing at him, and still, in her numbed condition, losing the battle.

In a few minutes, he not only had her out of her coat, but stripped down to her underwear. She should have been mortified; instead she was furious.

"Get away from me, you jerk," she snapped, and tried to grab back her shirt to hold in front of her.

"I'm not looking to get lucky here, Kyra." His voice was clipped and just as furious as hers. "I'm trying to keep you from getting frostbite."

Great. A man finally sees her in her brand-new matching, red lace bra and panties, and it's only because he's trying to play doctor. Yes, she was icy-cold right down to her bones. But she'd have preferred keeping her wet clothes on than to be undressed and ignored by Garrett Wolff.

"By stripping me in a freezing cabin? Good thinking, Einstein."

"God, you're a pain in the ass," he muttered, and pushed himself to his feet. Grabbing a blanket off the back of the closest chair, he wrapped it around her, and through the fabric briskly rubbed her arms and back, trying to speed up her circulation.

"*I'm* a pain in the ass?" she countered, refusing to admit, even to herself, how good it felt to have him rubbing the iciness out of her skin. "*I'm* not the one pushing *you* around."

"I'm not the one acting like a spoiled infant when someone's trying to help her."

"Infant?" She slapped his hands away, shoved at his chest, then drew her knees up and wrapped the blanket around her as tightly as she could. Pointless as it was now to try for dignity, she gave it a shot, anyway. "I wonder how you'd like it."

His features tightened and his mouth flattened into a grim slash of determination. "I'm sure I wouldn't. But just maybe I'd try to remember that whoever was ordering me around was trying to help."

Okay, maybe she was overreacting a little. But come on. What woman wouldn't have fought him on that? He'd stripped her down like she was a cranky two-year-old! The fact that she wasn't nearly as cold as she had been didn't really matter. Sure, he'd helped. But it was the *way* he'd helped she was taking issue with.

"You're thinking."

"Is that against the rules?" she snapped.

"Not if it keeps you quiet," he told her.

"Nice. Very nice." Then her eyes widened. "What the hell are you doing now?"

"I'm getting me warm again." He stood up, undid his shirt buttons and tossed the soaking fabric to one side. Then, while Kyra watched, he stepped out of his shoes, took off his socks and pulled his slacks down and off.

She couldn't stop looking at him.

It had been like opening a badly wrapped present to find something fabulous inside.

His chest was broad and tanned, with a sprinkling

of curly blond hair drifting down across his flat, muscled abdomen to disappear beneath the waistband of his dark blue boxers.

He was built like a cover model, and Kyra hoped to God she wasn't drooling.

Grabbing another blanket from the end of the sofa, Garrett wrapped it around his shoulders, then sat down in front of the fire beside her. Glancing at her, he asked, "What?"

"Nothing," she said, shaking her head as she tried to ignore the flutter of something hot and twitchy deep within. "Nothing at all."

"Good," he said flatly, his tone all-business. Then reaching out, he grabbed her frozen feet and pulled them onto his lap.

"Hey!"

His big hands closed around her ankles and she felt heat pool beneath her skin.

"Shut up, Kyra."

Muttering under his breath, he rubbed first one foot, then the other, stroking, kneading, using his strong fingers to rub away the last of the cold. His hands were warm, his touch gentle, despite the fury still crouched inside him.

As her body relaxed and her brain went limp, Kyra willingly shut up and allowed herself simply to feel.

Chapter 8

Didn't seem to matter how icy her skin was, Garrett felt on fire just by touching her.

He shot her a glance from the corner of his eye. She was leaning back against the stone hearth, the fire right behind her, gilding her in a halo of heat and light. His mouth went dry and his pulse quickened until the racing of his own blood was nearly deafening.

Shifting his gaze to the flames themselves, he tried not to think about what she'd looked like when he'd stripped her out of her business clothes. Pale, creamy flesh, red lace bra and panties, long legs and sleek lines, curves and tempting valleys. His heartbeat thundered in his chest and he told himself to get a grip. They weren't in this cabin on some lost-weekend getaway.

They'd been stranded in a storm.

Now they were trapped together.

Two people who otherwise wouldn't have willingly spent more than an hour in each other's company.

Besides all that, she worked for him.

What he was feeling was completely inappropriate.

And totally overwhelming.

Every inch of his body was on full alert. Restraining the urge to keep from sliding his hands up her legs, over her hips, to cup her breasts was taking every last ounce of his near-legendary willpower.

Who would have guessed that Kyra Fortune was hiding red lace underwear beneath her woman-in-charge power suits? And how would he ever be able to sit across from her in a meeting again without wondering what other delights she was hiding?

"That really feels good."

Her voice was a purr of satisfaction and did something to him that he really didn't want to think about.

He swallowed hard and tried to keep his voice brisk, businesslike. "Looks like you don't have to worry about frostbite, anyway."

"Lucky me." Edging away from the hearth, she

stretched out on the rug. But she kept her feet in his lap, lifting them into his hands.

"Yeah," he said. "Lucky."

"The fire feels great."

"Seems to be plenty of firewood here," he said, struggling to keep his brain focused away from the fact that her feet were now rubbing against a part of his body that didn't require any more encouragement. "Once you're warmed up, I'll go check. There's probably more in back."

"What about you?"

He risked a quick glance at her, saw her eyes fixed on his face. "What about me?"

She propped herself up on her elbows, tipped her head to one side and watched him. "You're making sure I'm all warmed up. But you were out in the snow, too."

"Trust me," he said tightly. "I'm plenty warm."

"Really?"

Speculation rang in her tone and Garrett figured it was time to stop the massage. Things were getting a little too intimate here, in the firelit darkness. "I'm fine, Kyra." He set her feet down on the rug, then stood up and looked around the cabin.

Shadows filled the corners of the room, but the candles and fire provided enough light to let him see that the place was well taken care of. Probably some city dweller's weekend retreat. Thank God it was here. Otherwise, they'd have been screwed.

"I'm going to check for more firewood. Why don't you look around, see if you can find a phone that works or something?"

"Okay." She rose slowly, stiffly, gathering the edges of her blanket around her like a shield.

But it was no use. He'd already seen what she was hiding. The images were burned into his brain. Turning from those thoughts, he walked away from her while he still could.

The hiss and crackle of the flames was a soft counterpoint to the storm raging outside. He walked through the small kitchen, ignoring the cold that reached for him. Cold was better. Cold would help him restrain the impulses raging within.

Snow clouded the glass panes on the top half of the kitchen door. Bracing himself, he opened the door far enough to be able to see onto the back porch. As he'd hoped, there was enough stacked firewood to keep them warm for days if need be.

But God, he thought, as he clenched his teeth against the stinging snow that slapped at him. How was he supposed to keep his hands off Kyra when all he wanted was to bury himself inside her?

He welcomed the frigid air and the swirling snow he'd tried to escape just an hour ago. Right now the fires blazing inside him were more dangerous than the cold.

He wanted her.

More than he could remember ever wanting anything before.

Garrett shut the door and leaned his forehead against the icy glass. It didn't help. The kind of fires burning inside him wouldn't be quenched by snow or ice.

This kind of flame would consume him.

Kyra wore her blanket like a toga, with one end tossed across her shoulder. She'd found some clothes in the tiny bedroom off the main room, but she just couldn't bring herself to raid her benefactors' closet as well as their kitchen. So she'd make do until her clothes were dry enough to wear again.

It was clearly too late to worry about modesty, anyway. Garrett Wolff had already seen her in her underwear. She cringed just thinking about it, and tried to tell herself that at least she'd been wearing her new bra and panties.

Oh yeah. That was the good side.

How would she ever face him again at work? How would she be able to sit across from him in a meeting, and not remember that he'd given her one of the best foot rubs she'd ever had?

Oh, this just got more and more confusing all the time.

Dragging her mind away from the thoughts that were making her nuts, she focused instead on the lack of clothing and what she could do about it. For the moment, nothing.

But she had a suitcase filled with clothes back in the car they'd had to abandon. The storm couldn't last forever, she assured herself as she glanced out the kitchen window to the wall of white beyond the glass. Sooner or later it would stop and they could go back to the vehicle and retrieve the rest of their things. For now she'd use the blanket and be grateful.

Glancing down at the pot of soup bubbling on the propane stove, she gave thanks that they'd been able to get the darn thing lit. She'd camped a few times as a kid, but she'd never really gotten the hang of cooking over an open fire.

"Smells good."

She jumped, startled, and looked up at Garrett as he came into the candlelit kitchen. "You scared me."

One eyebrow lifted. "Forget I was here?"

Not likely, she thought. All she'd been thinking about for the last thirty minutes was how good his hands had felt on her skin. She kept imagining how those hands would feel on the rest of her, sliding up her body, tweaking, stroking, rubbing.

She cleared her throat and blanked her mind—at least temporarily.

"The pantry's pretty well stocked," she said, ladling the soup into two earthenware bowls she'd found in a cupboard. "There's enough food here to last us a month."

"Hopefully, we won't be here that long."

"I hear that," she murmured, picking up the bowls and carrying them to the small table set up under the windows.

"Thanks," he said, picking up a spoon and digging in. Between mouthfuls, he said, "When my clothes are dry, I'll go out back and see if there's a generator."

She studied him for a long moment in contemplative silence.

Finally, he looked at her. "What?"

"Nothing," she said. "It's just that I never would have figured you for the Daniel Boone type."

"I'm not saying I'm going out to hunt a bear and drag the carcass home."

"I know, it's just—" She broke off and ate a spoonful of the hot soup. She knew she was stalling, but couldn't seem to help it. It was hard to explain to a man—especially your boss—that you were seeing him in a whole new light. And that you found him attractive.

As the soup's heat spread through her, she said, "I only thought—"

"That I was born in a three-piece suit?"

"Not born exactly, but...yeah."

"Wrong."

He shrugged, and mesmerized, Kyra watched the play of muscles in his shoulders. When he spoke again, she had to force herself to pay attention.

"I grew up outside Longview. Little town."

She nodded. "I know where Longview is."

He smiled briefly. "We lived on about twenty acres. My folks worked hard, but there weren't a lot of...extras. We learned how to do without or to make our own."

"Your own what?"

"Whatever we needed."

"Like?"

He sighed and took another bite of soup. "Why so interested?"

"Humor me." She said it lightly, but Kyra *was* interested. More so than she would have thought. The man was a mystery. A thoroughly modern businessman, yet he knew his way around log cabins, generators and fireplaces.

"Not all that fascinating, I'm afraid." He shrugged again, as if distancing himself from the story he told. "My parents are from Sweden. We moved here when I was four. They bought some land outside Longview and grew vegetables they used to sell at farmers' markets."

He made it sound like nothing, but Kyra's mind drew a different picture. An immigrant family, working hard to make a life for their child. Funny, but she'd always assumed that he'd lived a privileged life. She wasn't sure why exactly. Maybe it was because that three-piece suit fit him so well.

But he obviously wanted to keep this light, so she asked, "And are you a good farmer?"

"No," he admitted with a smile that vanished almost as quickly as it appeared. "My parents could grow a crop on cement, but I didn't get the farmer gene." He finished up his soup, then sat back, the blanket he wore sliding down to pool around his waist. "I worked with them, saved what I could and put myself through college."

She imagined him as he must have been—young and handsome, filled with dreams that his parents probably hadn't understood. She wondered if they'd approved of him or if they wondered how they'd raised a man so different from them. She wondered if he was happy in his three-piece suit or if he ever wished his life were different.

And she wondered why she was wondering.

"What're your parents doing now?" she asked, more to keep her mind from straying down tangents than anything else.

"Still farming," he said with a slight frown. "I tried to buy them a place in Florida, let them relax a little, but neither of them is interested in retiring."

"At least you tried."

"They're stubborn."

"Okay, *that* gene you got."

He laughed shortly. "Look who's talking."

She smiled. "I admit I'm a little...tenacious sometimes."

"Like a pit bull."

"Thank you, that was lovely."

"Didn't say it was a bad thing."

Outside, the wind howled and spat snow at the windowpanes, hard enough to make them shudder in their frames. Out there, the world was white and cold.

Inside, the heat began to build.

There was an intimacy between them that probably would never have happened back in Red Rock. But here, trapped in a tiny cabin in the middle of a storm, they were forced to meet each other on common ground. It was as though the cabin was in a world separate from everything else. As if somehow the two of them were the only people in existence.

Kyra smiled to herself. Just two people in their underwear, trying to survive.

Shaking her head to erase the image, she told herself that the intimacy level they were reaching was just short of dangerous. Better to end it now, before things got even stranger.

She jumped to her feet and looked down at him. "I cooked, so you get to clean up."

He nodded. "Sounds fair."

Backing away from him, she said, "I'm going to take a hot bath." Then she stopped. "At least, I think I am. Is there hot water?"

He stood up, too, hitched his blanket into place, picked up the soup bowls and stopped. Kyra took a careful step back. He looked way too good.

In the candlelight, his tanned, sculpted chest seemed as if it had been carved in burnished copper. His features appeared harder, sharper than usual, and the air between them seemed to hum and crackle with anticipation. With hunger.

Kyra swallowed hard.

Garrett Wolff was her boss.

More, he was the boss who was probably getting ready to fire her.

There was just no way that sleeping with him could be construed as a good idea.

Her knees went a little wobbly at the thought and she instantly locked them into place.

"The stove's propane," Garrett was saying as he walked closer. "My guess is the hot water heater is, too."

"Okay," she said, backing up another step as he drew nearer. "Good, then. I'll, um…just go and…"

"Take a bath."

"Right!" She pointed her index finger at him and smiled, as if he were a contestant on a game show and had just come up with the answer that would win him a million bucks.

"While you do that, I'll bring in more firewood and wash the dishes." He walked past her toward the sink, and Kyra blew out a breath as he passed. Apparently, she was the only one feeling a little too itchy for comfort.

Gathering what dignity she could, while wrapped in a brightly colored woven blanket, she lifted her chin and left the room on legs that still felt pretty shaky.

But damned if she'd let *him* know how he was affecting her.

"Cold?"

"Nope," she said, and inched closer to the fire, cradling a glass of the red wine he'd found in the kitchen.

Garrett watched her covertly. Firelight danced on her skin, in her hair, giving her an almost ethereal beauty. She looked like some pagan goddess awaiting her worshipers. As soon as he thought it, he knew he'd line right up for his share of worshipping.

Hell, he wanted his hands on her again. He wanted to feel that soft, smooth skin beneath his palms. Wanted to take his time as he explored every curve and line. Wanted to bury himself inside her until nothing could tear them apart.

His body stirred, his blood pumped and he took a sip of the wine, hoping to ease the tension building within. As the rich, cool liquid slid down his throat, he turned to look at her again, bracing himself for the hunger he knew would slap at him.

He couldn't even remember the last time he'd wanted a woman this badly. With a need that clawed at his throat and scratched at his belly.

Scrubbing one hand across his face, as if trying to wipe away the images in his mind, he said, "While you were in the tub, I retried that phone you found in the bedroom."

"Anything?" She shot him a quick, hopeful look.

"Lines are still down," he said quickly, and watched disappointment bloom on her features. "Cell service, too."

He should have been disappointed, too. But damned if he hadn't felt a flash of gratitude when the phone was still dead.

"Oh. So we're really stuck."

"For a while, at least." And he wasn't sorry about

it. He glanced at the windows on the opposite side of the room. Outside, the storm still blew, the snow coming fast and furious against the glass. "At least until the blizzard's over."

Nodding, she sipped her wine before turning her head to look at him. "I didn't ever thank you for getting me through that hike from the car."

"You're welcome."

"And," she pointed out with a smile, "you owe me fifty bucks."

"What?"

"The bet, remember?"

Garrett frowned for a minute, then recalled how he'd challenged her to keep walking. He'd felt her giving up, surrendering to the cold, and he'd done whatever he could to keep her moving. Challenging Kyra was a sure way to get her to respond.

He slapped one hand against his blanket-covered hip. "Don't have it on me. Guess you'll just have to trust me."

She took another sip of wine. "I can do that, I suppose. After all, I know where you live."

"You do?"

"Sure." She grinned at him and her whole face lit up. "You live at the office."

He smiled ruefully at the truth in that statement. "Got me there. Although I'd like to point out that you spend just as much time there as I do."

"True."

"Why?"

"What?"

"Why?" he repeated, leaning toward the fire and carefully laying another log on top of the flames. As sparks billowed, then shot up the chimney, he turned his gaze back to her. Shadow and light played across her features and his breath lodged in his throat, almost strangling him.

"Are you asking as my boss or as my fellow snow-bound victim?"

Taking a gulp of his wine, he set the glass down on the hearth and reached for the bottle. Refilling his glass first, he then leaned over to pour her more.

He'd been doing some thinking about that very thing. With the two of them stranded here together, things were bound to get more…intimate than they normally would have on a standard business trip. And he was pretty sure he'd come up with the solution to this forced intimacy.

"How about a deal?" he asked.

"Depends. What kind of deal?"

She was a careful woman. And he admired that. "I say we agree that whatever happens in this cabin, whatever is said in this cabin, stays in this cabin."

"Meaning?" she asked, and he heard a breathiness in her voice that fed the fire burning inside him.

It was the only thing that made sense. He'd

worked it all out in his head while imagining her naked and wet in that old claw-foot tub. The two of them would be in close proximity for who the hell knew how long. If something should happen between them, then he wanted her to know and accept that once they got out of this place, they'd both go back to their own lives.

Covering his own ass? Maybe. Trying to protect her?

Yeah, that, too.

"Meaning," he said finally, "that while we're here, we're just Garrett and Kyra. There's no Voltage Energy. No employer, employee. Just two people waiting out a storm."

She considered his words for a long moment as she watched him carefully.

"Deal?" he finally asked.

After taking another sip of her wine, she trailed the tips of her fingers around the edge of the heavy glass. "Well, since you're my boss and you've already seen me in my underwear, I think, yes. It's a deal."

"And since you've seen your boss in *his* underwear, I think it's a good deal all the way around."

Lifting her glass, she held it out to him for a toast.

As he clinked his wineglass against hers, Kyra said, "To the storm. And to stranded strangers."

Garrett wondered if he'd just made things easier between them, or more difficult.

Chapter 9

Wine was a great ice breaker.

By the time the second bottle was opened, they were talking as if they were old friends. Knowing that whatever happened in the cabin stayed in the cabin gave both of them the chance to let down their guard.

"So," Kyra asked, holding out her glass for Garrett to refill again. "Your parents are still living in Longview?"

"Yep." He stretched out one hand to his slacks, checking to see if they were dry. "Still wet," he muttered, then looked back at her. "My folks don't want to leave the farm."

"And that bothers you?" She saw a flash of emotion glitter in his eyes despite the cool tone of his voice.

"No, I…" Bothered him, no. Worried him, yes. They'd sacrificed a lot for him over the years and now that he was in a position to help, they wouldn't let him. Pride was a hard thing for a son to fight. Especially when he understood it so well.

"You want to make their lives easier," she said for him.

It surprised him that she understood without his having to explain it to her. But why should it? Kyra had family, too. And for the first time he wondered what that family was like. He'd seen the picture on her desk, of her and her siblings. A part of him envied them.

"Is that so wrong?" he demanded, even knowing that she wasn't the person to ask.

"Only if it's not what they want," she said softly.

He shook his head and took another sip of wine as the small burst of anger he'd felt a moment ago slipped away. She was right, he knew. And the more he pushed them to accept help, the more stiff-necked they became. "It makes me crazy," he admitted finally. "I try to give them money, they won't take it and then there's a battle." Shaking his head again, he said, "They tell me they already have everything they want. They won't take money from me. Won't let me help."

"Stubborn."

He snorted. "You have no idea."

"At least they love you." The words were out before she could stop them. Wincing, she shrugged when Garrett looked at her, a question in his eyes. "Did I say that out loud?"

"Yes." He saw vulnerability in her eyes. A wistfulness that made him want to comfort her. And that feeling was suddenly so real, so urgent, he tightened his grip on the wineglass to keep from reaching for her. "Want to elaborate?"

"Not really," Kyra hedged, wishing she could rewind the last couple of minutes and delete that little slipup. She was much more comfortable talking about his family than her own.

His parents frustrated him, but she'd seen the look on his face when he spoke of them. There was real affection there. Love. It had always been there for him—and when love came that easily, people tended to take it for granted. A fact of life.

He probably didn't even realize what a gift it was.

And just how much other people would give to experience it.

"Oh, come on," he prompted. "We've talked about my family. So tell me what it was like growing up as a Fortune."

A Fortune. Kyra knew what most people thought of the Fortune family. A big name in Texas. Lots of money, power, influence. At least, she thought, for some of them.

"Not what you'd expect."

His brow furrowed. "Explain."

She sighed, recognizing that Garrett Wolff was not a man to back away from a subject. He would keep asking until she talked, so she might as well get it over with.

Taking a fortifying sip of wine, she said, "My branch of the Fortune family tree was just a little less stately than the others." Another sip of wine and she felt the warmth hit her stomach and spread through her veins.

Taking a breath, she started talking, slowly, reluctantly. This was not really the kind of story she enjoyed telling. But somehow, here in this firelit cabin, the problems with her family seemed a long way off. "My father was a banker. Successful." At least in his work. "But at home, he was a bitter man and he made sure all of us knew it."

Garrett was quiet for a long minute, as if considering just what his reaction should be. "And your mom?"

"Skittish." Kyra sighed as she said it and realized that once she got started, it wasn't so very hard to talk to Garrett. Maybe it was the concern in his eyes.

Maybe it was the quiet way he just sat there and listened. "Mom learned early how to stay out of range of my father's temper."

"He *hit* you?" The sudden outrage in Garrett's voice warmed her as thoroughly as the wine.

"No," she said quickly, giving him a smile as a reward for the protective streak that had popped out. "At least, he didn't hit *me*." There it was, she thought. The whole sad story of her childhood. Because she'd escaped her father's temper, his outbursts, she'd been separate from her siblings. She'd been different. And that had been almost as hard to live with as the misery her siblings had faced.

"I was the youngest," she said, committed now and having to finish it. "By the time I showed up, my father was already a miserable human being. Because of him, my sister and my brother Daniel left that house as soon as they could. My mother moved around like a ghost, trying to avoid attention, pretty much leaving her children to fend for themselves when it came to dealing with my father. And my brother Vincent…" she broke off for another sip of wine.

Kyra couldn't believe she was saying all of this. Couldn't believe she was telling Garrett Wolff, of all people, her deepest, darkest secrets. Was she out of her mind? Was she drunk?

She thought about that for a long minute and tried

to objectively judge her sobriety. And she had to admit that the slight buzz she felt didn't qualify as drunk. She was clearheaded enough to know what she was saying. She just couldn't figure out why.

But it was too late to turn back now.

"Your brother Vincent…" he repeated.

She swallowed hard and tasted the bitterness of acknowledging that she'd been responsible, however unwillingly, for making Vince's life far harder than it had had to be.

"Vince stayed," she whispered, running the tip of one finger around the rim of her wineglass, her gaze locked on the ruby-red liquid. "He stayed in that house, with my father, because of me."

"Kyra—"

She lifted her gaze to Garrett's, not caring now if he could read the guilt stamped in her eyes. "He protected me. Stood in front of me when my father went into one of his drunken rages." She inhaled sharply and blew the air out in a rush. "He remained in that prison of a house to save me from the man who should have loved us."

Guilt blossomed in her chest and gnawed at the edges of her heart. "He put off his own life until I was through high school and leaving for college."

"A good man," Garrett said softly. Then he asked, "Where are your parents now?"

"Dead." One word. Harsh. Stiff. She couldn't

leave it at that, though. "They died several years ago in a car accident."

"I'm sorry, Kyra."

She nodded and took another sip of her wine. "My father was driving. We never found out if he was drunk that night, but the smart money says he was."

"At least you still have your brothers and sister."

"Yeah," she said softly, "I do. Thanks to Vincent, we'll always have each other."

Her gaze locked on Garrett, and she noted idly that his image was suddenly wavering. She needed a second or two to realize it was because her eyes were filled with tears.

She blinked them back and said, "I owe him everything, Garrett. Everything I am, everything I've done, is because Vince gave me the chance. *That's* why I'm always at the office so late. *That's* why I work so hard. I have to prove to Vincent, to everyone, that I was worth the pain he endured."

Frowning now, Garrett blurted, "Do you think your brother needs proof? Do you think he wants some kind of reward for protecting his little sister? Do you really believe that's why he did it?"

"Doesn't matter why he did it," she argued. "The point is, Vincent sacrificed everything. For me." The burden of that one truth settled onto her shoulders with a familiar weight. One she couldn't shrug off. "I have to work twice as hard to be the best," she said, then suddenly remembered that she hadn't told him her good news from before they'd left for this doomed business meeting. "I signed the Hartsfield account today."

"You did?" He smiled at her and Kyra basked in it for a second or two. "That's great. Congratulations."

"Thanks," she said, then continued quickly, "I worked hard to get that account. Because I can't fail. If I fail, if I can't make it at Voltage, despite all the work, despite everything Vincent did for me, then what? What was it all for?"

"You're not failing at Voltage," he told her.

"Really?" she said, her disbelief clearly sounding in that one word. "Then why the early review?"

He shifted his gaze to the fire, and Kyra noticed his jaw tighten as if he was clenching his teeth. Well, so they weren't supposed to talk about work. He'd started it, hadn't he?

"Garrett…" It felt odd, calling him by his first name, when he'd been "Mr. Wolff" for so long. But what was stranger was that—she liked it. "What do you mean?"

"You're getting a promotion."

"A—" She stopped, snapped her jaw shut, then took a gulp of wine and let that information settle in. Once it had, a flash of irritation swamped the self-congratulations happening inside her. "You didn't want to tell me."

He looked at her. "No, I didn't."

All of the warm, fuzzy thoughts she'd been having for him a few minutes ago dissolved like sugar in water. "You let me think you were going to fire me."

"Yeah," he agreed. "I did."

"For heaven's sake, why?"

Sighing and shaking his head, he sipped his wine, then turned his gaze on her. Shrugging, he said, "Because you irritated me."

She laughed shortly, but the sound scraped the air, and ached as it left her throat. "I irritate you?"

"You used to."

"But not anymore."

"Not until now, anyway."

"Oh, well, color me relieved." Kyra didn't know what to make of this. Sure, she was happy about the promotion. Happy she hadn't let Vincent down. Let herself down. But there was something else here. Something she couldn't quite put a finger on.

"You wanted me worried," she accused.

"Maybe I did," Garrett said, and let his gaze drop. In the firelight, his features looked sharper, harder. "You're always so damn sure of yourself, Kyra. It can be...frustrating."

She'd heard that before, and because she realized the truth in it, she said, "I'm not as confident as I let people think I am."

Not easy to admit, but since they were opening up here, talking about things that would never come up in conversation anywhere else, she felt as though she owed him at least as much honesty as he'd just given her. "I learned a long time ago that sometimes, if you act like you're right, it's almost as good as being right."

She'd brazened her way through college and steadily climbed the corporate ladder with the same game plan. Confidence equaled success. She knew that. So instead of letting the world in on her own self-doubts, she covered them with a layer of arrogance and hoped no one noticed.

"I can understand that," he said softly, his words almost lost in the hiss and crackle of the flames. "And I get why you're working so hard to make your brother proud." He smiled again briefly, sadly. "I do the same thing. My folks worked themselves half to death to make sure I had a shot at the American Dream, whatever that is. I can't let them down."

"But you haven't. You *are* successful," Kyra said, somehow moved to try to make him see himself as she did. Well, at least as she saw him now. "You're at the top of your game. Voltage's fair-haired boy."

"At the moment," he acknowledged. "But how much will be enough? How high do you have to climb before you say, 'Here's good. This is the top. Now I can relax'?"

She sighed and shifted position, curling her legs up under her and smoothing her blanket to cover her ankles. "I don't know. Maybe no one does. Maybe there is no magic spot on the ladder. Maybe it's just working every day, doing your best and hoping someone notices."

"Should that be enough?" He let his head fall back and stared up at the fire-lit ceiling. Almost as if talking to himself, he said, "I saw you doing all the things I used to do when I first went to Voltage."

"What do you mean?"

Still he didn't look at her, and his voice sounded… tired. "You work too much, Kyra. Stay too late, devote too much of yourself to the company. You put the job before everything else." Without lifting his head, he glanced at her. "Trust me. That's no way to live."

Something inside her cracked just a little and she felt a tension she'd been carrying around with her for years ease up slightly. "Maybe I have been a little single-minded."

He chuckled.

She scowled, then smiled, silently admitting his point. "Fine. A lot single-minded."

"Is the job all you want?" he asked.

"Never really thought about it." Ridiculous, but true. She'd been so focused for so long, there hadn't been room in her life for anything else. Her friends had fallen away, except for Isa. Her dates were so infrequent, Kyra might as well be living like a nun.

And now that she thought about it, she couldn't even remember the last time she'd done something as simple as go outside during the day. Always, even on most weekends, she was locked away from the world, tucked in her office, struggling to become the kind of success that would make Vincent's sacrifices worthwhile.

Frowning, Kyra wondered when she'd taken the turn in her own personal road. The one that had brought her to this lonely little spot. Success had always been the goal. But she'd never really stopped to analyze the cost.

Yet even as that thought zipped through her brain, she reminded herself that no cost would be too high to repay her oldest brother for the gift he'd given her.

The gift of a childhood.

The gift of innocence.

Silence stretched out for several long minutes. The storm raged and the fire hissed. The shadows in the room lengthened, reaching out to the circle of light where Kyra and Garrett sat, suddenly closer than they had ever been before.

How strange it felt to be here with him and feel this connection to a man she'd thought her enemy. Even stranger to look at him and feel her insides quiver with want.

"I've got another question for you," Kyra said finally, when she couldn't stand her own treacherous thoughts another second.

He laughed shortly and checked the level in the wine bottle. "If this keeps up, we may need another bottle."

Kyra cupped her glass between her palms. "I'll risk it."

"Okay. Then shoot." He took a sip and waited.

"As long as we're delving into each other's dark, demented pasts, I'd like to know something else. Something I've wondered about."

"Consider me warned. Ask away."

She couldn't believe she was going to pose this question. But what better chance would she ever have to get the answer to something that had been niggling at her for years?

"You were engaged…."

"Twice," he stated.

"Yet you didn't marry either of them. Why?"

His mouth tightened, then as if he'd made a conscious effort, relaxed again. "Lots of questions around the proverbial water cooler, huh?"

She nodded. "There was some speculation."

"And the consensus was?"

How much honesty could one night take? she wondered. Then she decided to go for it. They were both already in this so deep, what was another inch or two? "That the fiancées in question couldn't break through your wall of ice, and just ended things."

He smirked, drew up one blanket-covered knee and rested his forearm atop it. Kyra deliberately kept her gaze focused on his face.

"The truth is," he admitted, his voice dropping to a notch just above a whisper, "fiancée number one was just looking for a fast dive into my bank accounts."

"Cold," Kyra muttered.

"Oh yes," he agreed. "Fiancée number two was a much better actress." He stared hard into the flames, as if seeing into his own past. And judging by the expression on his face, he didn't much care for the images.

"She convinced me that she wanted to be a wife and mother. That she loved me and wanted the same things I did."

"And...?"

He shrugged. "She lied. The reality was," he said, shifting his gaze to Kyra, "she was a convicted felon. She took a job at Voltage, hoping to embezzle from both the company and me."

"Whoa." Stunned, Kyra just looked at him, unsure of what she could possibly say. His jaw muscle twitched as if he was gritting his teeth, and who could blame him? Someone he'd trusted had turned on him in the most awful way possible.

"Thankfully," he said, reaching for the wine bottle again, "I found out in time."

"How?" The word slipped out before she could stop it. Instantly, she knew she should have.

He looked at her sharply. "Does it matter?"

"No," she acknowledged, noting the flash of old hurt in his eyes. She really wanted to be able to step back in time and slap the woman who'd done that to him. "I guess not."

He blew out a breath. "I didn't find out the truth myself. Carol did."

"The pit bull?"

Smiling slightly, he said, "Yeah. Apparently, she didn't care for number two and ran a little background check on her. She told me what she'd found."

Okay, Carol Summerhill just went up another notch or two on the creepy factor. What kind of woman sneaked around behind her boss's back and investigated his fiancée? Even if the woman did turn out to be a thief. Wasn't he a little concerned about Carol?

"Did you know she was doing that?"

"No." He bit the word off, then softened his reaction by adding, "There were a lot of things about Carol I didn't pay attention to until you showed me. Carol is…"

"Territorial?" Kyra suggested.

"In a word."

There were several other words she could use to describe his admin, but Kyra figured now wasn't the time. If he was paying closer attention to the woman now, he'd find out on his own that Carol was not only crazy about him, but probably just plain crazy.

Kyra added quietly, "I'm sorry, Garrett."

"About what?"

She lifted one hand, let it fall. "About those women. The lemons you picked in the garden of love."

He laughed shortly. "Don't be. When it was all over, I realized that I hadn't really loved either one of them. I was more in love with the idea of what they represented. My heart wasn't hurt. Just my pride."

"Sometimes that can be worse."

"Yeah. I guess it can."

He refilled his glass and poured more into hers as well, before setting the bottle down onto the hearth again.

"Why'd you want to get married, anyway?" she asked.

"Interesting question," he said, one dark blond eyebrow lifting. "Don't you?"

A sharp jolt of laughter shot from her throat and she slapped one hand across her mouth. "God, no."

Curiosity replaced the old pain in his eyes as he watched her. "But isn't a marriage and a family part of the whole American Dream?"

"For some, probably," Kyra said flatly, feeling a rush of carefully banked temper begin to flare inside. "For me, no. The real American Dream is living your life the way you want to. Making your own choices."

He laughed. "Hey, don't hold back, Kyra. Tell me how you really feel."

"You asked," she reminded him, but smiled because now his blue eyes were clear again, free of remembered pain and disappointment.

"I did. So tell me why marriage is not for you."

"It's a trap," she said, before she could think of a way to say it just a little more gently. "I mean, maybe it works for some people, but for me getting married only means that I'd be taking on someone else's expectations. Their problems. Their dreams. Their demands."

"You can't judge all marriages by your parents'."

"It's really the only model I have to go by." She lifted her glass in salute and took a sip.

"No one else you know? No other family members who've had good marriages?"

Instantly, she thought of Lily and Ryan, and a warmth scuttled through her. Those two really did have the kind of marriage that most people dreamed of. But how many people ever found what *they* had?

"My brothers and my sister have all recently taken

that step, so I'll hope for their sakes that they get the kind of marriages they deserve."

"They're willing to risk it, but you're not?" he asked quietly. "Even though you said yourself that you never really had to go through the mess they did with your parents?"

"I watched it," she said, remembering snatches of ugliness, raised voices, swinging fists, crashing vases. Shaking her head, she said again, "No. Not for me. I'm not going to give a man that much power over me."

"It shouldn't be about power."

"You're right," she said, tipping her head to one side to study him. "It shouldn't be. But all too often, it is."

"So, because you don't want to get married, you live your life at the office," he said, leaning toward her until he was close enough that Kyra shivered, hoping he'd come even closer. "Isn't that a little lonely?"

Firelight danced on his face, making his eyes sparkle and shine with hidden promises. Kyra's stomach flipped weirdly and her heart did a strange little two-step before settling down again.

She licked her lips and let her gaze drift to his mouth, then back up to his eyes again. Something was happening. She felt the change. The shift in conversation. In tone. In his body language.

And oh, she really liked the language it was speaking.

"I didn't say I was against sex. Just marriage."

One corner of his mouth lifted. "Glad to hear it."

He reached out and took her wineglass from her, then set both glasses on the hearth.

Kyra's heart pounded hard in her chest, slamming against her rib cage until she thought it just might fight its way free of her body altogether. Her mouth suddenly bone dry, she watched in anticipation as he turned back to her.

Cupping her face between his palms, he stroked her cheeks with the pads of his thumbs and said, "I'm very glad to hear that."

His mouth brushed hers once, twice, a gentle testing, tasting. Then he pulled his head back and stared into her eyes as if giving her a chance to back out. To call this off.

Nothing could have been further from her mind.

"Mr. Wolff," she whispered, leaning in to kiss him once, then twice, as he had her, "if you don't kiss me in the next ten seconds, things are going to get ugly."

He smiled. "Wouldn't want that."

Grabbing her, he yanked her tightly against him, tipped her head back and took her mouth in a kiss that set the ends of her hair on fire.

Chapter 10

Flash fire.

Those two words erupted in Garrett's mind the moment his mouth touched Kyra's.

The world stopped.

His brain shut down.

Instinct took over.

He laid her back on the braided rug and pulled the blanket from around her body with the eagerness of a kid diving into a long-awaited Christmas present.

She pulled him down, wrapping her arms around his neck, holding him tightly, pressing his mouth to hers. Tongues danced, breath mingled, desire flared.

Again and again he tasted her, swallowing her

sighs, taking her breath, giving her his. She met him stroke for stroke, her desire more than a match for his own.

Better than wine, the taste of her filled him and effectively closed out everything else. There were no thoughts but to have her, no wants that weren't centered on her.

He broke the kiss, leaving them both gasping for more. But kissing wasn't enough. Pulling back, he reached for the front closure of that red lace bra he'd been thinking about for hours, and quickly unhooked it.

She sighed again as her breasts spilled free, and Garrett's heart jittered to a stop in his chest. "You're gorgeous."

Kyra laughed, and her whole body shook with it as she reached up to touch his face lightly. "Don't sound so surprised."

He grinned at her, feeling a rush of something that was more than desire. More than anything he'd ever experienced before. "Not surprised," he finally managed to say, "just pleased."

"Now, that's nice," she said, and let her hand drop to her side again.

"Oh," he assured her, "I'm just getting started."

Her skin felt like silk—smooth, creamy silk. Firelight shifted across her, light and shadow defining every curve, and he couldn't look at her enough.

His hands swept up and down her body, needing to touch, to feel, to explore her flesh, learn its texture.

For years they'd worked together, he mused, his mind racing. The tension between them had always been there, alive, active. They'd buried it in work. Ignored it by keeping their distance.

Now, though, it wouldn't be denied.

Now it was exploding.

"I have to have you," he murmured, dipping his head to take first one nipple, then the other into his mouth. His lips and tongue and teeth tortured her and she writhed beneath him. Soft groans and sighs buffeted the air, echoing inside him with the ferocity of howling need.

Holding his head against her breast, she arched against him and whispered, "I need you, Garrett. Now."

"Yes," he muttered, his voice muffled against her body. "Now." He couldn't wait. Couldn't torture either of them any longer. If he didn't have his hands on her in the next few seconds, he wasn't sure he'd survive.

He slipped from her grasp, pulling back and away from her, despite her protests. In seconds, he had them both out of what was left of their clothes.

"Now," he agreed, swooping in for another kiss, another exchange of heat, promise, anticipation.

She smiled up at him, licked her lips and nodded. "Oh, yeah. Now."

Grinning fiercely, he reached for her wrists. Bracketing them both in one strong hand, he held them tight over her head and used his free hand to skim her body.

"No fair," she murmured, twisting again, turning into him, straining to pull her hands free, to touch him as he touched her.

He dropped a kiss on her mouth, shook his head and said, "Let me feel you."

His right palm slid down the length of her body, following her curves, skimming across her abdomen and closer to her core, her center.

Her eyes opened wide and she went still in his arms, her gaze locked with his. She hissed in an expectant breath.

He didn't disappoint her.

His fingertips pushed lower, lower, until he could feel the damp heat of her drawing him in. Smothering a groan, he watched her face. As he stroked her most sensitive spot, her features tightened and her summer-blue eyes glazed over. But it wasn't enough. He wanted her clamoring for release.

Again and again, he caressed her, teasing, taunting, pushing her higher, until her head tipped back while she strained against his hold.

Turning in his grasp, pumping her hips in a frantic rhythm, she raced toward an explosion that shivered just out of reach. Garrett wanted to watch her reach it. Wanted to see her eyes go hazy and soft, feel the whisper of surrender in her body.

He wanted to be the one to take her higher than she'd ever been before.

Still keeping her wrists bound together in his grasp, he dipped his head and took one of her nipples into his mouth.

She groaned his name with a sigh of need, nearly wept, and the soft sounds she made fired his own desires even higher.

He fed the urge within. He suckled her, drawing and pulling on her nipple as she pressed close, losing herself in the moment. And while he tasted her, he pushed first one finger, then another into her damp heat.

He stroked her, inside and out, and felt the quivering of her bunched muscles. With her body primed, her back bowed, she pushed closer, trying to take his fingers deeper.

"Garrett…" She spoke his name with a heavy sigh. "I want you inside," she whispered. "I want to feel you inside me."

He gritted his teeth and still managed to say, "Not yet. First I want to watch you. I want to see you shatter."

A brief smile appeared and then was gone again in a rush.

"Come on, Kyra," he murmured. "Fly for me."

He felt the end draw close, felt her mounting tension.

She planted her feet on the rug beneath her, lifted her hips into his caress and cried, "Garrett…"

His name on her lips sounded like music. He stared down into her eyes and watched the storm clouds gather there. She was so close, so close and still fighting to keep that satisfaction at bay.

"Go over," he demanded, and kissed her hungrily. Mouth to mouth, breath to breath, soul to soul.

When he pulled his head back to look into her eyes again, he muttered thickly, "Let go, Kyra. Let me take you to the top. Let go."

She shook her head wildly from side to side. "I don't want it to stop. Don't want it over."

He laughed, a strained, harsh sound. She was so stubborn, he thought. About everything. This woman affected him like no one else ever had. "It's not ending, damn it. It's just beginning. Go, Kyra. Go over now."

She did.

Her body tightened, her hips rocked and she shrieked his name as he pushed her so high the only choice she had was to fly.

He released her wrists before the last of the tremors coursed through her. She reached for him, pulling him down on top of her, wrapping her arms around his neck and drawing his mouth to hers. "Amazing," she whispered between short, hard kisses. "Just amazing."

He agreed. His own body felt as tight as a bow string, yet satisfaction rippled through him at the same time. Just watching her climax had given him more pleasure than he'd ever expected.

Feeling the connection with her, watching passion glaze her eyes, hearing the hitch in her breath— all of it had touched him more than he'd ever been touched before.

Yet now he wanted more. He wanted to bury himself inside her, feel her heat surround him, take him in.

"Your turn," she whispered, as if reading his mind.

She cupped his face in her palms, kissed him brainless, then pushed him over onto his back. Garrett stared up at her and saw the dangerous glint in her eyes. It should have made him nervous, he supposed, but he was too busy enjoying himself.

She scraped her bloodred fingernails along his chest, tweaking his flat nipples until darts of sensation shot through him like mini lightning bolts. Sliding one leg across his body, she straddled him, sitting up straight and staring down at him like some warrior princess.

Firelight touched the strands of her hair, sang along her skin and painted her in shifting patterns of light and shadow. She was mesmerizing. He couldn't stop looking at her. He knew that if his gaze shifted, his heart would stop.

She smiled, a proud, knowing, female smile that sent more electrical shocks racing through him. Outside the cabin, wind howled and icy cold reigned. Blurring day and night together. The storm blotted out the sun and nature's power was supreme. Here the power was Kyra's.

Here she was the center of the world.

He reached for her, his hands coming down on her hips, his grip tightening as he felt the urge to hold her fiercely enough so that this moment would never end. That he would always be able to keep her here, in this one fraction of time, with the firelight playing on her body.

But she wouldn't be captured.

Shaking her wispy blond hair back from her face, she went up on her knees, rising over him like the morning sun climbing in the sky. His heart hammering in his chest, Garrett locked his gaze on her. He slid his hands higher, higher, until he could cup her breasts with his palms. Then she covered his hands with her own and smiled at him.

"Your turn now," she whispered, her voice almost lost in the crackling of the fire. "Watch me take you."

He couldn't have done anything else.

Slowly, so slowly she damn near killed him, she lowered her body onto his. Inch by tantalizing inch, she took him inside her, drawing out the action until he felt his brain dissolving.

Garrett clenched his jaw and fought for control, though it was a losing battle. His thumbs and forefingers tweaked and pulled at her nipples. Her hands, still covering his, moved with his touch, following every motion, touching herself as he touched her. And every movement she made raised a blistering fury of need that grabbed him by the throat and squeezed.

Still she moved slowly, lazily, as if deliberately trying to push him beyond the edge of sanity. And Garrett suddenly didn't care anymore. Sanity was overrated, anyway. He groaned as she finally completed her task and his body filled hers.

"You're killing me," he warned in a broken gasp of sound.

"*So* not my intention," she said, smiling. Then she moved on him, rocking her hips, rubbing herself against him. She swiveled slightly from side to side, creating friction, more tension and more desperation.

His hands dropped to her hips as he instinctively tried to set the pace. But she wouldn't be rushed.

"I'm taking you this time," she whispered and slid her own palms up and down her body with long, sensuous strokes designed to drive a man wild.

"You are," he managed to say, and kept his gaze focused on her as rivers of sensation coursed through him, carrying him higher, faster than ever before.

Kyra watched him watch her, and felt her insides go warm and liquid even as her body tightened around him. He filled her completely. Having him locked within eased all the dark, lonely corners inside her. She'd never known anything like this. Hadn't known she could feel so much.

Her heartbeat quickened; her breathing came shallow and fast as her body tightened expectantly. She rocked her hips, taking Garrett as deeply as possible. She looked into his eyes and lost herself in those stormy blue depths.

Moving on him became instinctive, looking at him became all important. Feeling his hands on her was more vital than her next breath.

"Come with me," he whispered, his voice a harsh rasp of sound that rolled along her spine and settled deep in the pit of her stomach. "Fall with me, Kyra. Together this time."

How could she not? It was as if their bodies had already become one, linked on more than just the physical level. She felt him touch not just her flesh, but her soul.

He'd looked into her heart tonight. Heard about her family, her childhood, her secret wants and needs, and he'd understood. He'd listened, and really heard her. What greater magic was there?

"Together," she said softly, keeping her gaze focused on his. Leaning forward, she linked her fingers with his. Bodies locked, they raced toward completion together.

And together they fell into a shower of sparks.

In Red Rock, Texas, Lily Fortune stepped out of her bedroom and quietly shut the door behind her. Just for a moment she leaned back against the door and closed her eyes, wishing she could change things with the power of her love.

But there would be no miracle this time.

No magic.

The life she and Ryan should have had together was ending far too early, and there was nothing she could do about it.

He was slipping away from her. She felt it. Sensed it. With every second that ticked past, Ryan was more and more a part of the world that lay beyond this one. She couldn't hold him here, despite how very much she tried.

Pain pulsed low and deep inside her, reverberating with every beat of her heart, and Lily knew that the slow, solemn music of it would always be with her.

Because when Ryan finally left, he'd be taking her heart with him.

"Mrs. Lily?" Rosita Perez, housekeeper, confessor and friend, approached warily, as if afraid to speak too loudly. Rosita was a little thicker around the middle than she used to be, but her dark eyes, filled with warmth and understanding, were the same as always.

Sighing, Lily forced a smile she didn't feel, and knew that the other woman wasn't fooled by it. "I'm all right, Rosita."

"Mr. Ryan?" The woman's gaze slipped past Lily to the closed door and back again. Anguish shimmered in her eyes, as if she already knew the answer to her question and dreaded having to hear it spoken aloud.

"It's time," Lily said, pushing away from the door and standing up straight. She lifted her chin and brushed away a solitary tear that streaked along her cheek. As hard as this was, she wouldn't let Ryan down by falling apart now. She would make it through the next few miserable hours, and then find a quiet place where she could grieve alone for the love of her life. "Call his children together. Call everyone."

Rosita's wide, dark eyes filled, but she only nodded jerkily and turned for the stairs.

Alone again, Lily stood in the late afternoon sun-washed hallway and faced the coming emptiness with a heavy heart.

It took about a half hour for the paralysis to ease.

Every muscle in Kyra's body ached, even a few she'd never been aware of before. But on the whole, she felt good. Too good.

Reaching for their wineglasses, Kyra took a drink from hers as she handed the other to Garrett. He propped himself up on one elbow, took the glass and drained the ruby liquid in one long, thirsty gulp.

Kyra's mouth watered as she watched him, and she had to wonder how this had happened. How had they gone from enemies to friends to lovers all in the span of one day?

And now that so much had changed between them, how were they supposed to handle it?

"You're thinking again," he said. "I can almost see the wheels in your mind turning."

She didn't deny it. What would be the point? "There's a lot to think about."

"Yeah, I guess there is." He set the glass down on the floor beside him and sat up to face her. "But before you start thinking too much, I want to say I'm not sorry that happened."

"Oh," she said with a quick, rueful smile, "me neither. It might be easier if I were sorry. Then I could call it a mistake and forget about it."

"Is that what you want?"

"No," she admitted. No sense in lying about this. "I don't want to forget about it, but I don't know what to think about it, either. So I guess I'm feeling confused more than anything. But sorry? No. Hard to be sorry about something that was so great."

Yet even as she spoke, she reached for the blanket she'd come to think of as her toga. His hip pinned it to the floor, though, and as she tugged it free, he grinned.

"A little late for modesty, isn't it?"

She flipped her hair back from her face and clutched the blanket in front of her. It didn't really matter that her backside was still naked. "It's not modesty. I know it sounds silly, but this is different. When we're naked and…busy, it's okay. When we're naked and chatting, it's weird."

But she hoped he wouldn't feel the same. It would be a shame to have him wrapped up in a blanket again. She really liked looking at his body, hard and muscled and oh, so very talented.

A hum of something nearly electrical buzzed through her and Kyra sucked in a gulp of air.

"You should know," she blurted, before she could

think better of it, "this whole, spontaneous sex thing is so not like me."

"I figured."

"Oh, really. Why's that?"

"Hell, Kyra. You're at the office practically twenty-four hours a day. When do you have time to be spontaneous?"

"Good point. But I just wanted you to know that this was out of character for me."

"Well then," he said, grinning again, "my congratulations. You're damn good at it."

She smiled, then shook her head. "I'm trying for serious here."

"Right."

"It's not that I don't like sex. It's fine. Warm and comforting and nice enough."

"High praise indeed," he said wryly, reaching for the wine bottle.

"Not you," she said quickly. "I was talking about the other times. Not so many, either, because I don't want you to think I'm easy or anything. Not that I'm a prude, by any means. But I don't want tonight to give you the idea that I'm all about 'Call Kyra for a good time,' because that's not who I am, either, you know?" Oh God, she was babbling again. Words flew from her mouth like water rushing from a broken dam.

There didn't seem to be any way to stop herself.

Her mouth was in full throttle. Neither could she avoid looking at his eyes and watching them widen as she just kept talking. Oh, God, could a person actually die from embarrassment?

"And I think you should already know all of that without me having to tell you because you've actually known me for years, and if there's the slightest chance that you're going to lose all respect for me because of this…" She gestured with the wineglass and sloshed some of the liquid over the rim and down her hand. "Then I have to remind you that you're my boss, for heaven's sake, and respect runs two ways and—"

Garrett leaned in and kissed her. He was figuring out pretty quickly that the only way to shut her up when she was on a roll like this was to give her mouth something else to do. Something he was more than happy to help her with.

After a few long, amazing minutes, he pulled his head back to look at her. A faint smile curved her lips, and her eyes were hazy with renewed passion.

"Was that a blatant attempt to get me to stop talking?"

"Oh, yeah. Did it work?" he asked, taking her glass to set it aside, then grasping her hand and slowly licking the wine from her flesh.

She shivered, blew out a shaky breath and admitted, "Oh, yeah. It worked great. Now, do you think you can stop me from thinking, too?"

"I'll do my best," he promised, and tugged the blanket away from her truly gorgeous body.

"Well," Kyra said, leaning into him and wrapping her arms around his neck, "I happen to be in a position to know that your 'best' is really, really good."

"You ain't seen nothing yet," he promised and pulled her down on top of him.

Chapter 11

This time it was even better.

Kyra's mind fogged over as Garrett smoothed his palms up and down her body. The man had patience. He didn't leave a single square inch of her skin unexplored. He used his hands, his fingertips, to drive her body higher, higher.

Her vision swam and she had to fight for breath.

All she could focus on was Garrett and the magic of his touch.

He kissed her lazily, languorously, as if he had all the time in the world. As if he wanted to taste her as he would a fine wine, the subtle scents and textures. His mouth was an instrument and he was a maestro.

His tongue swept over hers, sending tingles of anticipation through her that settled low in her belly. Her own tongue explored his mouth, the warmth, the intoxicating depths of him. Chills raced along her spine, and her heartbeat quickened until the furious thump of it filled her ears, deafening her to all but the thunderous pounding.

Firelight played on his features as he pulled back from her and let his gaze travel up and down her body with the same thoroughness as his hands.

"I can't seem to see enough of you," he admitted, reaching to stroke his fingertips across her abdomen.

Her stomach muscles quivered and she arched into his touch, wanting more, wanting everything.

"I know just what you mean," she said, enjoying the shift of light and shadow across his bare, muscled chest.

He smiled at her and Kyra wondered why she'd ever thought him cold and distant.

The man who was with her now was just the opposite. Warm, giving, a generous lover. He was sure enough of himself to be able to laugh during sex, and confident enough in his own masculinity to enjoy himself when Kyra took the lead.

She'd found more in Garrett Wolff than she'd ever expected. Found more in herself when she was with him than she'd ever expected.

But she would think about all of that later, consider what it all meant another time.

At the moment all she wanted was more of him.

More of what happened when they came together.

Garrett shifted position, moving to kneel between her legs, and Kyra's breath caught in her throat. A swirl of something hot and needy pooled in her belly and her mouth went so dry she couldn't even swallow.

She reached one hand toward him. "Garrett—"

He caught it in one of his. Smiling at her, he shook his head.

"My turn again," he whispered, then turned his face into her palm and kissed it, nibbling at her skin with the edges of his teeth. She shivered, closed her eyes and sighed.

"This is so not fair," she murmured, bracing herself for the sensations she knew were just about to start.

"Who said anything about being fair?" he asked, and scooped his hands beneath her bottom, lifting her off the floor.

"You're an evil, evil man, Garrett Wolff."

"And you like it," he countered, lowering his head until his breath gently dusted her most sensitive flesh.

"Oh, yeah. I really do," she confessed, staring into his eyes, letting him see the hunger wracking her.

"Just what I wanted to hear." Then he stopped talking, lowered his head and took her heat with his mouth.

Kyra hissed in a breath and instinctively rocked her hips into his kiss. His tongue swept over her flesh, smooth, soft, silky. He teased her, tasted her, taunted her, and she hoped wildly that he'd never stop.

Heart pounding wickedly in her chest, she lifted her legs to his shoulders and gave herself up to the unrelenting crash of sensations. One after another they slammed into her, pushing her higher, faster, than she'd ever been before.

Never had she felt anything like this. No man had ever taken her so intimately. So deeply.

No one had ever touched her in so many ways.

No other man had ever touched her heart with such deadly accuracy.

His big hands kneaded her behind, squeezing, exploring. His tongue stroked her again and again. His lips and teeth worked her innermost flesh, tantalizing her with fresher, wilder sensations every second.

Kyra struggled to breathe. Struggled to hold on, to keep the release clamoring inside her at bay. She didn't want him to stop. Didn't want this to end.

Blindly staring at the ceiling, she watched, mesmerized by the play of light and shadow on the broad, wooden beams and planks overhead. From outside, the sigh of the wind sounded, and beside her, the fire still crackled with a cozy warmth that seemed to wrap the two of them in a separate world, one where only touch mattered. Where senses were filled and tomorrow didn't exist.

Then she shifted her gaze, looking at Garrett.

She couldn't take her eyes off him. Watching him as he took her was somehow even more exciting than the act itself. She reached for him, stroking her hand through his hair, holding his head to her. "Garrett, I feel…"

Everything, her brain whispered. She felt it all. Absorbed it all. And knew without a doubt it would never be enough. Even while her body prepared for another rocking climax, Kyra knew the hunger for him wouldn't end.

She would only want him more.

He groaned and stroked his tongue across the tiny nub at her core. Lightning bolts shot through her body, leaving her shuddering, gasping, poised on the edge of an explosion that would surely shatter her.

He used his tongue skillfully, caressing that one small piece of flesh again and again, feeding on her sighs, reacting to her hissed breathing and pants of need.

And when she couldn't stand the sweet torment any longer, Kyra surrendered to it. Still holding him to her, she shouted his name and allowed herself to splinter into a wild burst of colored light.

And while her body still shuddered in release, he laid her down, covered her body with his and slid inside her. He entered her swiftly, surely, impaling her with his length, filling her to completion.

Kyra wrapped her arms around him and held him to her tightly, scraping her hands up and down his broad back, scoring his skin with her nails. "Again," she murmured, tucking her face into the curve of his neck, kissing him, nibbling the base of his throat. "Again."

"Yes," he muttered, his voice a sharp scrape of sound.

"Garrett," she whispered, "take me now, and this time come with me."

He lifted his head to look into her eyes. "You touch me, Kyra. More than anyone ever has."

He dropped his head to take her mouth in a hard, fierce kiss. Then he stared into her eyes and watched passion flare as he rocked his hips against hers.

She groaned and locked her legs around his hips, pulling him even deeper within. Deep enough that she hoped he would never be able to find his way out again.

His hips rocked again and again, setting a rhythm that was as fierce as the emotions jolting back and forth between them.

She matched him move for move, stroke for stroke. Their bodies slapped together and the sound was earthy, elemental. Here, Kyra thought, here was what she'd waited for most of her life. Here was what she'd been missing.

Her body felt eager, alive, ready. It seemed that she was always ready for him. A look. A touch. Anything from him could spark this overwhelming need engulfing her.

And though a part of her was terrified of what she was feeling, Kyra was honest enough with herself to admit that she'd given up on finding this kind of magic long ago. And now that she'd found it, she intended to enjoy it for as long as she could.

Because it wouldn't last. She couldn't allow that.

This was the one special man who could breach her defenses.

This one man could have the power to hurt her.

She pushed those thoughts away. She didn't want to think. Didn't want to plan or worry or fret. For now she wanted only to feel. To surrender herself to him. To what the two of them could create, she and this amazing man.

It was amazing, Lily thought, through her grief. As she looked around at the faces of those gathered in Ryan's bedroom, she could actually feel the outpouring of love surrounding her.

They'd come to say goodbye. To show Ryan that death couldn't end what he'd begun.

Moving closer to the wide bed, where the man she'd loved for most of her life lay dying, Lily fed on the strength of their family. She drew on it, knowing that it would be enough to get her through this last, most difficult journey.

Ryan lay so still. Lamplight splashed across the brightly colored quilt that covered him. His breathing was shallow now, slowing until she counted seconds between each one. From outside, she heard birds singing and the wind sighing through the trees. Life was going on all around her.

Even though her own was ending.

Gently, she sat down on the edge of the bed and reached for one of Ryan's hands. Behind her, Ryan's daughter Victoria sniffled and muffled a sob. The woman's brothers, Matthew and Zane, and her twin, Vanessa, were all here with their children.

"Mom?" Lily looked up, responding instantly to her son Cole's concerned voice. "Is there anything we can do?"

She reached for his hand and squeezed it, then shifted her gaze to encompass everyone there. "You're doing it," she said softly, looking from one to the other of the sober faces clustered around the bed. "Just by being here, you're doing everything you can."

Then Lily forgot about everyone but Ryan. Turning back to him, she studied his familiar face and wondered why he could look so much like himself. His features were still handsome, still darkly tanned, and his thick black hair still made her fingers itch to touch it.

When his eyes opened and focused on her, she forced the smile she knew he would want.

"Lily." His fingers twitched against hers.

His eyes were clear for the first time in days. There was no more pain clouding their inky depths. He glanced briefly at his family, gathered close, and worked his mouth, trying to find the strength to speak. When he managed it at last, there were only three words for them to cling to.

To remember.

"Love each other," he whispered, his voice a faint echo of what it once was.

Lily crumpled, holding his hand tightly to her breast, as though if she held on long enough, hard enough, she might tether him to this world. To her.

She watched his eyes and saw the light slowly fade. He slipped away in inches, a quiet exit from a life lived so thoroughly.

When the silence in the room became a living, breathing thing, Ryan smiled and whispered suddenly, "Pa?"

Then he was gone.

* * *

Snow was still falling outside, and Garrett approached the window warily, almost as if he expected the drifts to spill through the glass. Wearing his now dry clothes, he leaned on the window frame and tipped his head to see the black sky above and the white flakes drifting from it.

The storm had lasted hours already and showed no signs of stopping. Hell, if this kept up, they could be stranded here for days.

As that thought occurred to him, he glanced over his shoulder at the woman sleeping curled on the rug in front of the fire. Not necessarily a bad thing, he conceded as his body reacted instantly, going hard and needy in the space of a heartbeat.

Straightening up, he scraped one hand across his face and tried to get a grip on the rampaging desire galloping through his system. Damn it, he hadn't reacted to a woman like this since he was in high school, trying to coax Sandi Brewster into the back seat of his dad's Buick.

Shoving his hands into his pockets, he strolled barefoot back across the cabin. Then he hitched up his slacks and squatted beside Kyra. Her wispy blond hair lay in uneven fringes around her face, making her look like an exhausted pixie.

Firelight shimmered on her skin, creating a rich glow that tempted him to touch. But he curled his fingers into his palm to keep from giving into that urge. He'd already done enough instinct-following today.

Lifting his gaze to the cheerful fire, he stared unseeing at the flames dipping and swaying in the chill wind slipping down the chimney. His mind wandered back to just an hour or so ago, when he'd looked down into Kyra's eyes as their bodies joined. When he'd felt her surrender, and allowed himself to do the same.

He pressed the heel of his hand to his chest and rubbed, as if that motion could get rid of the nagging ache in his heart. But even as he tried, he knew he'd fail. Kyra had slipped inside him. Somehow or other, the woman who'd been a pain in the ass at work for eight years had become *important* in just a few hours.

But maybe, he thought, it wasn't as sudden as all that. Maybe this had been coming on for years. All of the arguments, the friction between them. Maybe it had all been leading them here.

"You look awfully serious."

Her quiet voice drew him out of his thoughts, for which he was grateful. Because despite what he was feeling at the moment, Garrett had no idea how they were going to handle this change in their situation.

"Still snowing," he said, and lowered himself to sit on the floor beside her.

"Wow." She glanced at the window, then looked back at him. "When Colorado has a spring blizzard, they do it up right."

He smiled and reached out to smooth her hair off her face. She rubbed her cheek against his hand and smiled back at him. "You got dressed," she said accusingly.

He shrugged. "Went out to get more firewood. Clothes seemed like a good idea."

She nodded and pushed herself up into a sitting position. Leaning back against his chest, she looked into the fire. "I didn't mean to fall asleep on you."

"You were tired."

She tipped her head and grinned at him. "Not tired. Exhausted."

Her smile caused a jolt of reaction inside him and Garrett wondered why he'd never taken the time to see past her cold, hard-at-work attitude before now. How could he have missed her warmth, her humor? How could he have been immune to the sexual pull of her direct, blue-green eyes?

And how the hell would he ever be able to ignore them now?

"Phone's still out," he blurted, trying to ease his mind away from thoughts that had no solution, questions that had no answers.

She nodded and nestled closer, dragging her blanket up to cover her breasts. "Then I guess all we can do is wait."

"Looks like," he said, feeling his body stir and thicken. His blood raced and his heart rate tripled, commencing an uneven, jackhammer beat.

She let the edge of her blanket dip a little, displaying the tops of her breasts and the sweet valley between them. "So," she asked thoughtfully, "wanna play some cards?"

"No," he replied, his gaze locked on her cleavage, just the reaction she'd no doubt been hoping for.

He'd always considered himself a rational, calm and collected kind of man. Funny how a few days with Kyra had changed all that.

But then again, maybe she hadn't changed anything about him. Maybe she'd just awakened something inside him that had always been there. Maybe he was simply becoming the real Garrett. The person he'd buried under work and responsibility all his life.

"Okay, then, how about a board game?" she teased. "I saw some over there on the bookcase." She lifted one hand to point and the blanket dipped another notch or two.

"I don't think so."

Deliberately, she dropped the blanket a little lower, and Garrett held his breath, waiting for her nipples to appear.

"Okay," Kyra said, tilting her head back to look

at him again. Licking her lips, she pulled the edge of the blanket down even farther, baring her breasts to his hungry gaze. "So, we could go in the kitchen and get something to eat?"

Shifting his gaze to hers, he reached out and cupped one of her breasts in his palm. His thumb stroked her hardened nipple and he smiled as she closed her eyes and sighed.

"I'm hungry," he admitted, amazed to feel the need clamoring inside him again, even fiercer than before. "But not for food."

She opened her eyes and looked directly into his. Reaching up, she curled one arm around his neck and pulled his mouth down to hers. "Show me."

Chapter 12

Kyra gave herself up to the incredible feelings Garrett aroused in her.

In her brief nap, her dreams had been filled with him. With the memory of his touch, the warmth of his breath on her face. Waking and finding him here, beside her, had stirred the dreams to life.

He cradled her close and Kyra listened to the steady beat of his heart beneath her ear. Through the thin fabric of his dress shirt, she felt heat streaming from his skin.

His hands moved up and down her body, sliding the blanket off as he gave himself free rein to touch, to define every line and curve.

She arched into him, amazed at the flash of renewed desire jolting her. How could this keep getting better and better? How could she only need more of him?

No man before him had ever made her want so completely. Had ever made her laugh or crazy mad or stirred such feelings of tenderness. Always before, she'd kept a part of herself separate. She'd been careful to maintain an emotional distance.

Maybe it was about control, she thought idly, while Garrett stroked her body. She'd seen firsthand, with her mother, how giving in to a wild attraction could ruin a woman's life. And she'd never wanted that for herself.

Until now, with Garrett Wolff, she hadn't had any trouble at all sidestepping the slippery slope of affection.

He laid her down on the braided rug and she smiled inwardly, knowing that there was a nice, soft bed in the other room and they'd never gotten that far. But what did beds matter, really?

Closing off the thoughts beginning to plague her, she stretched out under his stroking hands, like a spoiled cat searching out a spot in the sun. When he leaned back and stripped his clothes off, Kyra's breath caught in her throat.

Instantly, her brain raced with more questions that didn't have answers.

Where was it coming from, this overwhelming attraction? The fiery chemistry? For years they'd worked together, snarled at each other and in general done everything they could to avoid being in the same room alone together.

Was it because they'd each somehow sensed what would happen if there were no rules? No strict code of employer, employee? No real world intruding on them?

And what would they do when they had to leave this place?

She reached for him as he covered her, and forgot everything else in the rush of the moment. This time was slow, gentle. They came together in a hush of breath and unspoken promises.

He entered her on a whisper. Softly, smoothly, a quiet invasion, and her body welcomed him. Her heart suddenly full to overflowing, she took what he offered and gave all she had.

Their bodies moved in a natural, easy rhythm, as if they'd been together for years and knew each other's wants and needs. His hands were magic, his mouth a gift. He sighed her name and she felt a flash of something warm, amazing, ping inside her. Her eyes filled with tears and she closed them so he wouldn't see. Wouldn't misunderstand.

Wouldn't read in her expression what she was feeling.

With every caress, he delved deeper into her heart. Deeper into her mind. Her soul. Kyra knew it was happening and couldn't stop it. She wasn't even sure if she wanted to stop it.

She'd lived her whole life never looking for love, avoiding whatever situations might have led her to it. And now, when she least expected it, Love with a capital *L* knocked her for a loop.

As the wonder of that realization swept through her, Garrett kissed her and her heart soared. He murmured her name and Kyra felt more alive than she ever had before.

She clung to him more tightly, welcomed him more deeply, and this time, when the stars exploded behind her eyes, all she could see was his face.

Sometime later—who knew how long, since she wasn't wearing her watch?—he handed her her clothes and, smiling, said, "If we don't get dressed, whoever owns this cabin will find two very naked, very dead people when he comes back here."

"Not a bad way to go, though," Kyra said, already slipping her bra on and hooking it. She shrugged into her shirt, and as she buttoned it, she looked at him. "What happens in the cabin stays in the cabin, right?"

He glanced up from the row of buttons on his shirtfront. "Right. Just like Vegas."

"Then tell me something."

He stood up to step into his pants, then sat back down again before saying, "What?"

"Why now?"

"What do you mean?"

She sighed and shimmied into her panties. "You know exactly what I mean, Garrett." Swinging her hair out of her eyes, she grabbed her own slacks and brushed fruitlessly at the lint clinging to them.

"Okay, yeah, I do," he said, and drew one knee up to brace his forearm across it. "But I don't have an answer for you."

"Too bad. Neither do I," she admitted, and stood up, stepping into her slacks and zipping them up before sitting down on the hearth rug again.

"Does there have to be an answer?"

"Usually," she said, and wondered why it was so much harder to talk to him than it was to make love with him. What kind of weird situation was that?

"Maybe it was just circumstances and—"

"Please." She cut him off sharply and nearly smiled when his blue eyes narrowed. Love zinged through her again and she nearly laughed. She used to get furious when his expression went all stony. Now, heaven help her, she actually thought it was cute. "And don't make the annoyed boss face at me, either. Not here. Not now."

He scowled darkly for a second or two, then his

features cleared as he shook his head. "'Annoyed boss face'?"

"Yes. You know the one. Your eyes get all small and your forehead goes wrinkly."

He lifted one hand to his brow to check, then dropped it again. "I don't make faces."

"Yes, you do," Kyra countered, "but that's not really the point at the moment, is it?" Before he could speak, she charged on, full steam ahead.

"You were about to say that all of this—" she waved a hand to encompass the room and all that had happened between them "—happened just because we were stuck together."

"And it didn't?"

"You're telling me if you'd been stuck in this cabin with Carol, the same thing would have happened?"

"No." Clearly appalled at the thought, he frowned at Kyra again.

"Or how about Terry, Mr. Henderson's assistant? Would it have happened with her?"

"No, and I don't understand what you're getting at, Kyra. Nor do I see the point."

"The point is, it wouldn't have happened with me and anyone else, either."

"Glad to hear it," he muttered.

"Thanks. Me, too." He looked as confused as she felt. And why not? Neither one of them had come on this business trip expecting to discover what they'd found in this cabin. And she, at least, couldn't be more confused about how to handle it.

"God." His jaw dropped and his eyes went suddenly wide and horrified.

"What?" Kyra leaned over, covered his hand with hers and said, "What is it? What's wrong?"

"I can't believe this," he muttered thickly.

He shook off her hand and pushed himself to his feet. Then he paced back and forth across the room, muttering to himself in a voice so deep she couldn't make anything out.

Kyra watched him shove both hands through his hair, then drop his arms to his sides. Her stomach did a weird stop and spin as she wondered what was driving him. His steps were long and hurried, as if he were trying to escape from something.

An icy curl of dread settled in the pit of her stomach as she watched him. But she'd never been one to put something off. Better to just face it and get it over with. Figure out a way to deal with it.

"Will you stop the pacing and tell me what's wrong?"

He did stop. And when he shifted his gaze to hers, Kyra read fury in his eyes. Not to mention guilt. "What's wrong?" he repeated incredulously. "What isn't? I can't believe we did this. Can't believe neither one of us stopped to consider—"

She stood up, crossed to him and slapped one hand against his broad chest. "For heaven's sake, just say it."

"We didn't use any protection, Kyra. Not once." He grabbed her upper arms and yanked her close enough that she had to let her head fall back so she could meet his eyes. "I never thought of it."

This she could deal with. A part of her had worried he was about to say everything that had happened had been a horrible mistake. That he wished she'd never come on this trip. That he never wanted to see her again.

Then again, now that she was considering the implications, Kyra couldn't believe she'd been so stupid. Ms. Look-Out-For-Herself had simply thrown caution to the wind and gone with what had felt too good to ignore.

She was now officially a cautionary tale.

"Oh, boy." She planted both hands on his chest, felt the thud of his heartbeat beneath her palms and knew her own was a match for it. "I…"

"Right."

"We—"

"Oh, we certainly did."

Her brain raced like a runaway train headed for a washed out bridge. She'd never done anything so stupid, so careless in her life. She couldn't believe that she'd been so out of control, she'd forgotten the first rule of surviving dating in the twenty-first century.

Self-protection at all costs.

"Okay," she said, watching flares of temper flash in his eyes. "We were stupid."

"Oh, yeah." He viciously rubbed the back of his neck. "I'd say so."

"But it'll be okay as long as you're healthy."

He actually looked insulted. "Of course I'm healthy. Do you think I would have—"

He broke off, let go of her and took a step back. "Damn it, Kyra, I wouldn't have put you at risk that way."

"I appreciate it," Kyra said, taking a step toward him. "And you should know that I'm healthy, too."

One corner of his mouth lifted, but the half smile didn't reach his eyes. "Good for us. But there's still the possibility of—"

"No, there isn't." She cut him off neatly before he could even say the word *baby*. Hey, no point in calling down curses.

"You're sure?"

"As sure as taking the Pill can make me," she told him. "Granted," she added with a shrug, "they're not one hundred percent effective, but—"

"They're not?" He looked appalled again. "Isn't that their job?"

Kyra laughed. "Yes, but nothing is foolproof."

"Oh," he said, smiling grimly, "I feel better."

Obviously the thought of making a baby with her was more worthy of a freakout than the threat of disease. Well now, Kyra thought. Didn't she feel all warm and cuddly?

"Relax, Garrett. I'm not pregnant and I'm not going to be pregnant." Ever, she added silently, but he didn't have to know that. But she'd already told him how she felt about the prospect of getting married. Surely he could figure out for himself that she felt the same way about parenthood.

Sure, some single women made great mothers. And if it worked for them, that was terrific. But Kyra would want any child of hers to have both parents. And since she had no intention of getting married, that sort of left her out of the whole motherhood issue.

Although, with this newfound realization that she was actually in love with Garrett Wolff, maybe none of her resolutions were worth anything. Suddenly, without warning, an image drifted into her mind: she and Garrett, hands linked, smiling down at a cooing baby in a bassinet.

Wow.

How had she gone from anti-marriage and love to blurry-eyed dreams of happily ever after in a twenty-four hour period? That had to be some sort of record.

"Relieved?" she asked, leaving her fantasies where they belonged—locked in a corner of her mind.

"Yeah," he said, frowning. "Of course."

But he wasn't, Garrett realized. In fact, a part of him was actually disappointed.

Crazy.

It made no sense at all to be sorry that he and Kyra hadn't made a child. Only a week or so ago, he'd been firmly convinced that she was the most irritating woman on the face of the planet.

And yet somehow now he was looking at her as if she might be the one woman he'd been searching for all his life. He just didn't learn, that was his problem.

He'd thought himself in love before. Twice he'd proposed to women who had professed to love him. And twice it had blown up in his face.

Was he really going to take one night of incredible passion and try to build it into a relationship? Even if he was willing to take that risk again—to put himself on the line and actually tell Kyra that his feelings for her had changed—she wouldn't be interested.

She didn't want love. Or marriage.

Or him.

Not an easy thing for any man to admit, but there it was. She'd made herself clear. She didn't want the things he did. Just because they'd found an incredible passion together didn't mean that they were destined to stroll through eternity hand in hand. Besides, he wasn't about to risk humiliating himself again by throwing his heart at yet another woman who didn't want it.

Kyra was watching him, and damned if he could figure out what she was thinking. Usually, her emotions were plainly etched on her features. Naturally, now when he could really use a clue, she was a blank slate.

"You don't have to worry," she said, splintering the silence stretching between them.

"What?" Not what he'd been expecting. Though why that should surprise him, he couldn't have said.

"I said you don't have to worry." She tossed her hair back from her face, tilted her chin up and gave him a smile that wasn't the least bit convincing. "I'm not going to follow you around at work making puppy eyes at you or anything."

He shook his head as if to clear it, but that didn't help.

"We agreed," she was saying, "that what happens here, stays here, and that's just how it's going to be."

A flicker of irritation erupted inside him. "Business as usual, then?"

"We're two mature adults," she said firmly. "I'm sure we'll be able to handle the situation at work with no problem."

"So nothing changes." Why did that sound so impossibly sad? What they'd found here together deserved more, he realized. More than either of them was willing to give.

She didn't look any happier about that than he felt, but she nodded. "It's the only way, don't you think?"

He wanted to say no. He wanted to grab her, hold her, bury his face in the curve of her neck and tell her that he wanted everything between them to change. He wanted to dance with her again. Go on picnics with her. Take long walks in the moonlight.

But he couldn't.

They'd made a deal.

And maybe, in the long run, that would turn out to be a good thing.

Chapter 13

By late the next morning, the storm outside had died, but the one inside the cabin was just getting started.

With the power back on, the phone was working and so was the television. Its muttering voice had become an intrusion as newscasters gleefully reported on the disastrous snowstorm that had rocked areas of Colorado.

Garrett occupied himself with the news channels, and he and Kyra hadn't spoken more than a word or two to each other in hours. She missed the closeness they'd had the night before, the solidarity of the two of them surviving together.

Now the world was creeping up on them, demanding they pay attention to more than themselves.

And she didn't like it one little bit.

Sunlight reflecting off the banked snow pierced the cabin windows, so blinding Kyra had to shade her eyes just to look around the room.

Not much to see, she mused. Considering what had happened here, she thought the carpet should be steaming or at least singed. Instead, the place looked just as it had when they'd arrived the day before, frozen half to death.

They'd cleaned up. Garrett had swept out the hearth and stacked more firewood. He'd left a check for five hundred dollars on the kitchen table, along with a note thanking their benefactor for the use of the cabin.

Now everything was done.

All they had to do was wait for the cab they'd ordered to come and pick them up.

She walked to the front door, opened it and stepped out onto the porch. A brilliant blue sky stretched overhead, and a muffled roar in the distance heralded the arrival of snowplows, clearing the highway. She shrugged deeper into her coat when a cold, sharp wind whistled through the stand of trees surrounding the cabin and pushed at her—as if even nature were trying to keep her here. With Garrett.

Her insides tightened, released and then tightened

again. She was so incredibly tempted to admit to him that she didn't want to go to the business meeting. Didn't even want to go back to Texas.

All she really wanted was to stay here.

With him.

Thankfully, though, sanity prevailed, and she somehow managed to keep her mouth shut. Because frankly, what if she did say something like that to him? What if she spilled her brand-new feelings out at his feet and he wasn't interested?

What then?

God, how would she ever be able to look at him again, much less work with him?

But then, how was she going to be able to sit in meetings with him and *not* remember what it was like to cradle his body within her own?

Groaning, she lifted one hand and rubbed at the spot between her eyebrows. Life had just gotten so much more complicated.

"You okay?" He'd come up behind her soundlessly, and she jumped in surprise at his voice, low and intimate.

"Yeah," she replied, and wondered when she'd gotten so damn good at lying. "I'm fine. Just wondering when the car will be here."

"Soon," he said. "According to the news, most of the roads are already cleared and crews are working on the rest of them."

"Good," she whispered, her gaze fixed blindly on a distant tree. "That's good."

"Yeah," he repeated, and stepped out beside her on the porch. Leaning one shoulder on a newel post, he shoved his hands into his pockets and said, "I put a call in to the people we were meeting with. Explained the situation."

Nodding, Kyra told herself to keep her voice even, her emotions calm. Just as he was. "Since they live here, I'm guessing they understood."

"They did. We've postponed the meeting for a few weeks." He turned, braced his back against the post and said, "When the cab comes, it'll take us to the airport and we'll take the jet home."

Home. One little word that could somehow be either filled with everything that mattered, or be a reminder that you had nothing to go back to.

Because really, Kyra thought now, her brain racing as Garrett stood beside her in the sunlight, what was waiting for her in Red Rock? An empty condo. Twelve-hour days at work. No real friends beyond Isa. No family of her own. No one to love.

God.

She hadn't been looking for love, for pity's sake. Why was it that suddenly love was all that seemed to matter? And why, now that she'd found it, was it even further away from her than before?

"Kyra?"

She turned and looked up at Garrett. His blue eyes were a shade lighter than the post-storm sky, but they were every bit as vast and just as mysterious. "What is it?"

Did she sound as tired as she felt? His eyes narrowed on her and she hoped to heaven he didn't do something disastrous, like give her a friendly hug. If he did, she just might humiliate herself by clinging to him like a barnacle on the hull of an old fishing boat.

But he didn't reach out to her. He kept his hands stuffed in the pockets of his slacks, even while his gaze locked on hers. "I just wanted to say…"

His voice trailed off, letting her know that whatever he wanted to say wasn't going to get said. And maybe that was just as well.

If he apologized or something, she'd have to hit him.

"It's okay, Garrett," she said quickly, filling the silence that seemed suddenly so loud. "You don't have to say anything. I think we both said everything that needed to be last night."

"I think you're wrong," he said quietly. "But the hell of it is," he added, his voice dropping even lower, "I'm not sure what the right thing is."

"Well," she stated with a wry smile as she shifted her gaze to the tree line again, "that makes two of us."

* * *

Garrett glanced across the wide aisle at Kyra, who was curled up in the leather seat, hands tightly clenched, staring out the jet's window at the ground rushing past them.

Just as the night had rushed past them.

He wanted to go to her. To sit down beside her, pull her into his arms and admit that he didn't want to leave what they'd shared in that cabin. But to do that, he had to risk not only his heart again, but his pride.

And damned if he was willing to do that.

Not even to recapture what they'd had. What they'd found together.

The thought of never being with her again ate at him. But the idea of asking for more and not getting it was enough to keep him quiet.

The jet lifted off the runway, and Garrett leaned back in his seat with the pull of gravity. Soon they'd be home in Texas—where they lived separate lives—and this one little blip on the radar screen would be buried under the mundane details of working together.

His fingers tightened on the folded newspapers in his lap. Nothing to be done about it. They'd made a deal and he'd stick to it, whether he wanted to or not. He flicked her another quick glance, felt his heart squeeze in his chest, and knew that this would be the hardest thing he'd ever had to do.

Grimly focusing his concentration on anything but his racing thoughts, he opened the paper he'd picked up in the airport lounge. His gaze skimmed the headlines, then dropped lower, until just beneath the fold a line of bold black type caught his attention.

"Damn it," he muttered.

"What?" Kyra shifted in her seat.

"I don't believe this," Garrett said, and stood up, clutching the newspaper and focusing his gaze on the damning article. "How the hell did this happen?"

"Depends," she said, her voice even as she stood up and took the paper from him.

"Don't—" Garrett snatched at it, wanting to grab it back before she could see.

"Are you kidding me?" Her voice hitched until it sounded like a shriek.

"It's a mistake," he said, and this time he succeeded in taking the paper from her limp hands.

"Is it?" she demanded, snatching the paper away from him again, dropping her gaze to the article in question. "'Voltage Energy Company of Red Rock, Texas, is being investigated after accusations made by a disgruntled employee. The unnamed source claims to have proof that Voltage is conspiring to build an energy monopoly with Fortune TX, Ltd. Kyra Fortune,'" she read, her fury evident, "'a member of the Texas Fortune family, is considered to be a key player in the venture. As a newly promoted VP, she is allegedly serving as liaison between Voltage and her family's company.'"

"Kyra…" Garrett reached for her, but she stepped back quickly, never looking at him. Never taking her gaze from the folded paper she held in two white-fisted hands.

"There's more," she muttered darkly. "'When asked for a comment, Voltage CEO Miles Henderson was quoted as saying, "The investigation will come to nothing. Voltage has nothing to hide. And Ms. Kyra Fortune, a valued employee here at Voltage, has done nothing but excellent work."'"

"I knew Miles was up to something," Garrett said when Kyra's voice trailed off. "Why bring you into it?"

"Why would anyone do that?" she countered, finally lifting her gaze to his.

Garrett could have sworn he saw actual sparks shooting from her eyes. Every line of her body was rigid and a high flush stained both her cheeks.

"How the hell do I know why someone would do this?"

"Oh, I don't know," she said, tossing the paper down onto her seat. "You knew plenty of other things."

He braced himself, knowing that another storm

was coming and that this one would blow even colder than the blizzard they'd survived. "What's that supposed to mean?"

"You let me think I was going to be fired, when all the time you *knew* I was getting a promotion."

"All right, yes…" Right now he was wishing he hadn't played that game.

"And…" she said, stabbing her index finger into his chest, "you knew that I wasn't getting promoted because I earned it—which I sure as hell did—but because I'm a Fortune!" She waved a hand at the paper. "Henderson and the others wanted to *use* me to get to Fortune TX, Ltd. Didn't they? This was all a plan, wasn't it?"

"Yes," Garrett admitted, "I knew that the promotion was because of your name. But that's it. If there were other plans, I wasn't in on them. I suspected, but couldn't be sure."

But he'd for damn sure confront Miles Henderson the minute they got back to Red Rock. Garrett didn't like being used any more than Kyra did. And he had the distinct feeling there was a lot more to this monopoly accusation than he knew about.

"Damn it!" She threw both hands high and turned away to stomp down the wide aisle. When she reached the back wall, she spun around to glare at him. "I worked my butt off for that company. I worked nights, weekends. I got the big accounts. I've produced real results for Voltage and you know it."

"Yeah, I do," he countered. "You've worked hard, but so has everyone else." A quick flare of anger erupted inside him. Damned if he'd be accused of using her when he'd fought his superiors about the idea. "I was against this, Kyra. I didn't want them giving you that job this way."

"Or any way," she snapped.

"What the hell are you talking about?"

"Oh, please. You've been against me since day one." She walked back toward him, fire leaping in her eyes and danger pulsing off her like a thick, red aura. "You've shut me down any number of times. You don't take my ideas, you fight me even when you know I'm right."

"That's my job," he shouted, looming over her. She didn't flinch, and a part of him admired that, even when he wanted to grab her and give her a good shake. "I'm supposed to be the one to consider or reject ideas based on what I believe is best for the company. Not what Kyra Fortune believes. Because whether you want to admit it or not, you're not always right, Kyra."

"Oh, that's for sure," she said, a withering smile on her face. "I was wrong in thinking that last night would change anything. That maybe I'd misjudged you."

"Last night—"

"But I was right before," she interrupted, "back when I thought you were a pompous ass."

He scraped one hand across his mouth to keep from letting this degenerate into a mudslinging match. "I didn't know about the damn merger, Kyra."

"And I'm supposed to believe you."

"Why would I lie?" Fury licked at his insides and Garrett fought to restrain it.

"Why wouldn't you?" Then her voice dropped to a whisper, as if all the air had suddenly left her body. "My God. Did you really believe that I would go along with Voltage's plans to use me? To use my name?"

"Of course not. I told you I only suspected that."

She didn't believe him. He could see the distrust in her eyes, and he had no way to combat it. No way to convince her. So instead, he fought fire with fire, giving in to the temper crouched within. "You know, you've never made a lot of friends at Voltage."

"What does that have to do with anything?" she demanded.

"Maybe if you had, people wouldn't have been so eager to use you."

This time she flinched, and he had the dubious satisfaction of knowing his jab had hit home. Great.

Score one for him. He'd hurt a woman he cared about.

"Right." She turned away, dismissing him.

Garrett grabbed her upper arm and spun her around to face him. "That was a low shot. I'm sorry."

"Yes," she agreed snidely. "You are."

He sighed. "I'm not your enemy, Kyra."

Kyra looked up at him and saw a stranger. Her world was rocking and he was right in the middle of it. For years, he'd been her boss and he'd irritated her, annoyed her and infuriated her.

But she'd never thought of him as a sneaky, back-door kind of guy. She'd always felt that he was at least honest. Then last night she'd seen a whole new side of him. She'd discovered warmth instead of cold, fire instead of ice, and depth rather than the shallows.

Now, though, she didn't know what to think.

So she did what she always did when she was hurt. She attacked.

"Is that right?" Her voice was low, soft and full of venom. "Then why take me on this trip, Garrett?"

"What?"

"Why me?" she repeated, warming to the thoughts presenting themselves in her churning mind. "Why now? Tell me, was seducing me part of this whole deal? Did Miles tell you to show me a good time to make sure I went along?" Oh, God.

Pain lurched through her. Had she really been just a tool? Just part of a grand scheme to suck her family into a merger? Had nothing that passed between them the night before been real?

"Was this the plan all along?" she asked. "To make me pliable enough to approach the Fortunes on behalf of Voltage?"

He let her go as if his fingers were on fire. Staring at her through hard, cold eyes, he growled, "You know better than that."

"Do I?"

"You damn well should," he said tightly. "Last night was between *us*. It had nothing to do with either of our jobs."

"How am I supposed to believe that?" she asked, despite the ring of truth in his voice.

"Guess you'll just have to trust me."

"See, that's the problem," she snapped, "I *don't*." Reaching for the paper again, she shook it at him. "Trust got shot to hell the minute I saw this article, Garrett. Voltage was going to use me—so why should I believe that they weren't using you to get to me?"

Fury vibrated off of him in waves. His eyes were hot with indignation and his jaw clenched so tight she was surprised it didn't snap.

Watching his anger mount drained her of her own.

Kyra felt exhausted. Empty. Drained of everything that had so filled her the night before.

Then, she'd been truly, completely alive and just realizing that she'd fallen in love for the first time in her life.

Now she was faced with the sad truth that the man she loved didn't really exist. He was as much a fantasy as that one night in the cabin had been.

Shaking her head, she glanced down at the paper again. But this time her gaze drifted from the damning article about Voltage to the bold black print atop a different article, higher up on the front page.

"Oh my God." She swayed as tears filled her eyes and the world gave a sudden, hard tilt to one side.

"Kyra?"

She shook her head, tears falling freely now as she staggered back to her seat and fell into it.

"Kyra, what is it?"

Past the ringing in her ears, Kyra heard his voice, so soft and concerned. God, she wanted to curl up into his lap and find comfort. But there was no comfort for this. Nothing that could ease the pain.

And even if there were, she'd lost the right to turn to him. Lost that tenuous thread of shared affection. She'd had no idea that she would miss it so desperately, so soon.

She stared at the newspaper and read aloud the

words that had sliced her heart: "Ryan Fortune Dies at Double Crown Ranch."

A long moment of silence passed, where the only sound was the quiet growl of the jet engines winging them toward Texas. Toward a family battered by grief. Toward the emptiness of a quiet condo. Toward the promise of loneliness.

Then Garrett crouched in front of her and took both of her hands in his. "I'm so sorry, Kyra."

She let her head fall back against the seat. His grip felt warm, solid. But she knew this, too, was a temporary thing. This tenderness. Much like the night at the cabin, it would end once they reached their destination.

Better, she thought, that it end now.

"I know," she whispered, turning her gaze to the wide blue sky outside the window, "but it doesn't change anything, Garrett."

"Kyra—"

She couldn't look at him. Couldn't see sympathy in his eyes when she was still so disappointed in him...in everything. "Just leave me alone, okay?"

His hands tightened on hers briefly, then he let her go and stood up. "Can't I do something for you, Kyra?"

"You can get me home, Garrett," she whispered brokenly. "I just need to be home."

Chapter 14

Reporters had her condo staked out.

Kyra stopped her car at the end of the block and stared blankly at the crowd of people clustered in front of her home. News vans, antennae poking up from their roofs like antlers on deer, were double-parked in the street. Cameramen, photographers, reporters, all hungrily awaiting the story of Kyra's misery, jostled for space on the sidewalk in front of the gated entrance.

Driving straight here from the airport, all she'd been able to think about was closing herself up in her own home and drowning her sorrows in a glass of wine while sitting in a bubble bath. Now those plans were smashed. She'd never be able to get past that crowd unnoticed.

Closing her eyes, she rested her forehead on the steering wheel for a few minutes. Her heartbeat thudded painfully in her chest and she wondered just how much more could go wrong.

She'd lost her reputation, probably her job. She'd lost Ryan. She'd even lost Garrett—at least, the image she'd had of him for so short a time. God, last night felt like years ago. So much had happened so quickly. So much had been said, so many words spoken that could never be taken back.

She sighed and lifted her head wearily. Her heart ached from that last awful conversation with Garrett, and she felt more vulnerable at that moment than she ever had before. She couldn't help wondering why she'd ever thought that being alone was a good way to live.

Then she remembered the flash of anger and denial in Garrett's eyes when she'd accused him of using her, and told herself that maybe she'd been wrong about him. Maybe he hadn't known anything about this so-called merger.

But even if he hadn't, it was too late now to do anything about it. In her pain and fury, she'd lashed out at him—and she knew that part of the reason for her rage was that one sparkling moment last night when she'd realized that she loved him.

"What a mess," she whispered, and heaved a sigh that came all the way up from the tips of her toes. "What am I supposed to do?" she asked herself, more to hear the sound of a voice in the silence than anything else. "Where can I go?"

And just how sad was it that the one person she wanted to go to was Garrett—the one person she couldn't have?

Shaking her head, she swiped her fingertips under her eyes and muttered, "Get a grip, Kyra. You can't just sit here in your car for the rest of the day."

Suddenly she knew where to go. Whom to run to.

Still feeling emotionally battered and sorely disappointed, Kyra made a sharp U-turn and steered her car back the way she'd come.

Eyes teary, she blinked frantically to keep the road ahead of her clear. There was only one other place she knew she'd be welcome. One place that any Fortune in trouble could turn to.

She put her foot down on the gas pedal and headed for the Double Crown Ranch.

By late the next afternoon, all of Texas was buzzing about Voltage Energy Company and Fortune TX, Ltd. There were news vans camped outside Voltage and several at Kyra's place. Garrett knew because he'd gone by there last night looking for her, only to be told by frustrated reporters that she had never shown up at her house.

He'd tried calling her place to leave messages, hoping that she would at least dial in and pick them up. But if she had, she was ignoring him.

Garrett hadn't seen her since they'd landed at the private airstrip in Red Rock early the day before. She'd left word with her assistant this morning that for now she'd be staying at the Double Crown and not coming in to work. Garrett knew that even if she wanted to see him, he'd have a hell of a time getting past the ranch security. Especially now, with every dignitary in the country—and some from around the world—here for Ryan Fortune's funeral.

God, he wanted to see her.

Nothing had been the same for him since leaving that cabin. He wanted those hours again. He wanted to turn the clock back and reclaim the two of them as they'd been together. He wanted to be there for her now. To help her through the misery he'd seen glimmering in her eyes when she'd told him good-bye.

It killed him to know that he'd caused plenty of her misery himself. He should have told her the truth about the damn promotion the minute Henderson had ordered it. He should have trusted that anyone with Kyra's sense of self-determination wouldn't accept a promotion with strings attached. He should have—

Hell, he should have done lots of things differently. Should have opened his own eyes years ago. Seen that the friction between him and Kyra Fortune was a sign of the chemistry they shared. He should have risked his own stupid pride and his heart. He should have—

"Pointless to think about all that now," he muttered, parking his car in his reserved space at Voltage. "Lost chances are just that. Lost. What I have to do now is all that matters."

Last night, sitting in his empty house, he'd finally understood that to win back Kyra, he had to convince her that she could trust him. Now he just had to figure out how to do that.

He grabbed his briefcase from the passenger seat, slammed the door of his sporty convertible and headed for the gleaming glass building.

Since he couldn't reach Kyra at the moment, he was determined to focus his energies somewhere else. To find the truth behind the newspaper report. To discover what was real and what was fiction. Only then would Kyra listen to him. Believe him.

And Garrett knew, with sudden, heart-staggering clarity, that he wanted—no, needed—her to trust him again.

Because without trust, there could be nothing else.

And he wanted it all.

He'd been a damn fool and he knew it.

Gritting his teeth, he entered Voltage, nodded absently at the security guard at the front desk, then stalked past the lobby to the elevator. He pushed the call button and waited.

Here was his world. He'd given up his life, given up everything for this job. The one place where he'd made his mark.

For what?

Business?

Money?

"Bullshit."

"I beg your pardon, sir?"

Garrett blinked, glanced at the man standing beside him in front of the bank of elevators, and shook his head. "Nothing. Nothing at all."

"Right." The other man practically whistled as he turned his gaze away and studiously avoided eye contact.

Garrett hardly noticed. How could he? His mind was too filled with his own stupidities to think of anything else. He'd let Kyra go. He'd seen the pain in her eyes, yet he'd let her drive away on her own.

He should have said something.

But he hadn't, choosing instead to protect himself and his heart. From what? Claiming something amazing? A chance at the happiness he'd been searching for so long?

Idiot.

He stepped into the elevator, stabbed the appropriate button, then drifted to the back of the car, still thinking. He'd been afraid, he admitted. Too damn afraid to risk his pride by admitting to Kyra that he felt something for her.

Something? Damn it, even in his own thoughts, he was hedging. He straightened up at that realization. Hell, he could hardly admit it to himself. What the hell kind of coward did that make him, anyway?

"I don't feel *something*," he murmured, "I *love* her."

"Excuse me?" The same man half turned to look at Garrett.

"I wasn't talking to you," he snapped, a little embarrassed to be caught declaring his love to an almost empty elevator.

"Oh. Well who…?" He glanced around the otherwise empty elevator car.

"Don't you have some work to do?" Garrett demanded irritably.

"Sure. I mean, uh, yes, sir. You bet." He pushed a button on the elevator control panel, and as soon as the door opened, the man bolted.

When it closed again, Garrett paced the claustrophobic elevator like a tiger in a too small cage.

He loved her.

Why the hell hadn't he seen it? Admitted it?

"Why didn't I tell her?"

Idiot.

He leaned against the wall of the elevator and hit his head against it. So he'd have had to risk his pride. So what? What the hell was pride worth if he was alone and miserable?

No, he'd found something with Kyra, he realized as the elevator slid smoothly to a stop at his floor. When the door opened, he exited the car and, brain still racing, stalked past Carol's desk without a glance at her, to enter his own office.

He tossed his briefcase onto the closest chair and kept walking until he was in front of the wall of windows, staring out at the Texas sky. "It wasn't just one night," he murmured, wanting to hear the words aloud. "It was more. And with any luck, it could be everything. I have to tell her I love her. Make her listen."

"Mr. Wolff?"

Irritation leaped to life inside him. "I don't want to be disturbed, Carol," he said, not taking his gaze from the sweeping view in front of him.

He heard the door click quietly shut a moment later, so when he turned around to find the woman still in the office, he was surprised—and angry.

"Not now, Carol," he repeated.

His admin didn't move. Instead she stared at him through wide, horrified eyes. When she started toward the desk, her steps were shaky, as if she was having to force her body to function at all. "You *love* her?"

He scrubbed one hand across the back of his neck and fought for calm. "Carol, I think you should go back to your desk."

"I can't believe this," she muttered, shaking her head, keeping her stunned gaze on him in utter disbelief.

Garrett didn't have the time or the will to deal with Carol's little obsession. What had Kyra called her? A pit bull? "I'll buzz you if I need something."

"Did you sleep with her?"

Floored, Garrett blinked at her for a second or two. *"What?"*

"That slut, Kyra Fortune," Carol said, hissing the words through gritted teeth. "Did you sleep with her?"

Icy-cold rage poured through him like a tidal wave. Garrett glared at her and fought the urge to toss her out on her ass. "That's none of your business. I think you should leave, Carol. Now."

"You did." She snorted a harsh laugh and shook her head wildly. Her eyes were overbright and her mouth moved rapidly, though no words were coming out. Finally, though, she started talking again, and once she started, he couldn't shut her up. "Why would you choose *her* when *I'm* right here? Waiting for you?"

Whoa.

Garrett stared at the woman he'd thought he knew so well. She'd been an excellent assistant, organized, disciplined. And he'd never looked past that before. His fault? For not paying closer attention, yes. Realizing that mistake was the only thing that kept his voice cool and even.

"Carol…"

"I love you," she said, moving fast now to the edge of the desk, where she planted her palms and leaned toward him. "I've always loved you. Didn't I help you get rid of those other bitches? They were never good enough for you. I found out, didn't I? I saved you."

Her eyes were still wild, but there was something else there, too. Almost a feverishness. As if some control inside her had finally snapped and a dam had burst, releasing stored-up vitriol in wave after wave.

"Don't you see?" she said, coming around the edge of the desk, holding her hands out toward him, a greedy, grasping light in her eyes, "we belong together. It's always been just us. You and me. I can make you happy. I know how. You don't want that Fortune slut. Especially now."

A sense of protective fury ignited inside him at the slurs she was throwing at Kyra. But Carol was so far over the edge now, she didn't notice his anger. She was too wrapped up in her own need.

Garrett flinched at the irrationality in her eyes, but forced himself to listen, to get everything he could from her, though he wanted to give in to the fury rippling through him.

"Why especially now?" he asked, and grabbed her hands in both fists when she would have wrapped them around his neck.

She tipped her head to one side and gave him a beatific smile. "Because she's going to be arrested. I've taken care of it. She'll be a suspect in the monopoly charge," she assured him, her voice dropping to a conspiratorial whisper. "I told the reporter about the merger and the slut's promotion. I did it for you. She won't bother you again. I know how angry she makes you. Well, now she'll be fired. She won't be here to bother you anymore. To bother us. You can count on me. Always."

A sinking sensation flooded him. Carol had more problems than he could deal with, and truthfully, he didn't really care about her mental health. All he wanted now was to get to Kyra. To tell the government investigators what Carol had done.

But he needed proof.

"Carol, damn it, don't you know what you've

done?" he asked, though he already knew the answer. Of course she didn't know. "Thanks to you *I'm* going to be investigated, too. Because that reporter you fed your lies to took the story and ran with it. The man's built a house of cards out of half-truths and innuendos, and both Kyra and I are standing on top of it. Along with all of the executives here at Voltage." He gave her a shake. "Don't you get it? You've ruined me. All of us."

Her eyes cleared, focused, then welled up with tears. "That's not what I meant to do," she insisted, pulling her hands free of his and pushing them through her hair. "I only meant to help. To get rid of that bitch before she could hurt you like the others did. I love you, Garrett. I want to make you happy."

He shook his head in disgust and took a step away from her to keep from shaking her until her teeth rattled. This woman had caused so much trouble, it was almost hard to believe.

"I didn't mean to hurt you. I swear it," she said, tears coursing down her face, leaving black smudges beneath her eyes. "I'll do whatever you say to make up for this. I only want to help."

Garrett simply stared at her. She wasn't vicious. She wasn't even crazy. Just obsessed. And too willing to destroy others to get what she wanted. While he looked at her, broken now, crying softly into her hands, Garrett realized that there still might be a way out of this.

"There is something you can do," he said.

She looked up at him, her tear-streaked face shining in the sunlight. "Just tell me."

The funeral was officially over. The speeches were done, eulogies given, tears shed. There would be more tears, of course, because a man like Ryan Fortune deserved grieving. But for now the crowd moved toward the main ranch house, for a wake that would give the great man a real Texas send-off.

Kyra kept to the back of the mob headed for the house, and realized that she'd never seen so many Fortunes and Jamisons gathered together in one place. And all because Ryan Fortune had been such an extraordinary man.

A soft April wind ruffled her hair and plucked at the hem of her dark blue skirt. Her heels wobbled unsteadily on the river-stone path, and when she swayed, a hand grabbed her elbow briefly.

Looking up, she smiled wanly at Peter Clark, her cousin Violet's husband. Kind green eyes sparkled behind his glasses.

"Watch your step," he said quietly.

"Not so easy in these," she answered, pointing at the three-inch navy blue pumps.

"Heels aren't made for walking," Violet said from beside him. "They're for looking good."

He grinned at his wife. "And speaking for men everywhere, we appreciate your sacrifice."

Kyra smiled at the two of them as they moved deeper into the crowd. They were so good together, she thought, and they'd worked hard to build a life. Wasn't that what made everything worthwhile?

Mind whirling, she let her gaze drift over the others wandering past and around her. Clyde Fortune, a tall, gorgeous rancher, had one arm around his wife, Jessica, and Kyra paused a moment to think about all the two of them had overcome to find each other. Then there was Collin Jamison and Lucy. As she watched, Collin dropped a kiss on his wife's forehead and they looked at each other as if they were the only two people in the world.

Envy rippled through Kyra, and though she was ashamed of herself for it, she couldn't seem to stop what she was feeling. This was a day to remember Ryan Fortune's life. His legacy.

But wasn't love a big part of that legacy?

Love.

How could she ever have believed that she could live without love? How could she have been so blind as to push an emotional life to the side in favor of a professional one?

And now that she knew she loved Garrett, how would she ever get on with her life without him?

As the crowd neared the ranch house, music spilled through the open doors to welcome everyone inside. The bright, quick, happy beat of country music, with a fiddle and a steel guitar twanging in perfect accompaniment, charged the atmosphere. Already the mourners' steps were a little lighter, and the sadness lingering in the air a little less suffocating.

Kyra felt lost.

Lily had given her the use of the guest cottage on the ranch for as long as she wanted, and Kyra was grateful. She couldn't go home, not with reporters still lying in wait everywhere she went. Heck, she hadn't even called home to check her messages, not wanting to hear the rash of reporters pleading for a story. Besides, she couldn't bear the thought of returning to that empty condo.

Ever since that night with Garrett, being alone just felt more...lonely than before. Stupid. She'd fallen for a man who'd only used her to further his own ambitions.

Hadn't she? Yet even as she thought it, she wondered again. If that night of incredible passion had been an act, then Garrett Wolff was wasting his time in Texas. He should go to Hollywood and pick up an Oscar every year.

The truth was, she didn't know what to think, and that was making her crazy.

All around her, people whispered to each other, talking about Ryan, worrying about Lily. Kyra was surrounded by family and yet separate from them all.

What was Garrett doing now? Was he thinking about her? Missing her? Was he making a report to Mr. Henderson? Was he covering his own tracks with the investigation and leaving her out to dry?

And why did it hurt so much to think that he'd used her?

"Kyra?"

She looked up into her brother Vincent's concerned gaze. "Hi."

"You look a little out of it," he said, and bent to plant a kiss on her cheek.

"Good description," she admitted, then felt a stab of guilt because she'd been thinking about her own problems and not Ryan.

"Don't let 'em get to you, kiddo," he said, clearly referring to the newspaper reports. "Everyone knows you didn't do anything wrong at Voltage."

"Thanks." She gave him what she meant to be a quick hug. Then she was holding on to him, resting her cheek on his broad chest.

"Hey…" His big hands stroked her back. "Want me to go buy you some ice cream?"

She smiled against him and shook her head. "No, but thanks." Leaning back, she looked up at him and said, "But, thank you."

He frowned worriedly. "Kyra, you're going to be all right."

"I know. I just—" She broke off, then took a step back. "I want you to know how much I appreciate all you've done for me. I don't think I've ever said it out loud. But I want you to know how much I love you."

Embarrassed, he ducked his head, then guided her to one side of the moving crowd, where they wouldn't be overheard. "I love you, too, Kyra." He dropped a kiss on her forehead, then smiled at her. "And I'm damn proud of you. But all I've ever wanted was for you to be happy."

She blew out a breath and nodded. "I think I'm finally ready to be happy," she admitted. "Now all I have to do is convince the right guy that *he's* ready."

"My money's on you," Vincent said with a quick grin. "But if you change your mind and want that sundae after all…you just let me know."

"I will," she promised, already feeling lighter than she had in years.

"Now I'm going to find my wife. I'll see you inside, okay?"

"Right." She watched him disappear into the crowd, and fought that ripple of envy again as she realized that all of her siblings had found someone to love. Someone to be with. To share with.

Funny, but she'd never thought she was interested in the whole happily ever after thing. But in the span of a few hours in a snowbound cabin, she'd allowed herself to dream. To imagine. Only to have those fantasies shattered at her feet.

She moved forward again, walking with the crowd as she pushed her memories to the back of her brain and instead concentrated on the here and now. She couldn't do anything about the situation with Garrett or Voltage at the moment. But she could be a part of her family.

There'd be plenty of time later to plan a strategy for convincing Garrett that he loved her.

Ahead of her, country music rang out, and from somewhere in the crowd, a baby wailed, bringing life into the midst of death.

"You okay?"

Kyra came up out of her thoughts to smile at her sister, Susan. "I will be," she said as they climbed the steps to the open front doors.

"I still can't believe it," Susan said, draping one arm around Kyra's shoulders and leading her into the cool, shadowy foyer. "But," she added, looking around at the people streaming past them, "wouldn't Ryan get a kick out of seeing all these people show up just for him?"

Kyra smiled. The foyer was full of people laughing and talking.

Just one more instance of Ryan caring for others, even after death.

She drew a deep breath, the cool air scented with the rich, spicy Mexican buffet provided by Rosita for Ryan's friends and family.

Life pulsed on in a rush of sound and noise. Mourning would still happen, but the reality was that time stopped for no one. Not even a man as good as Ryan. Days would pass, grief would lessen.

But the memories would remain.

She heard the music, caught a snatch of laughter and the sounds of other people talking, sharing stories about Ryan. Remembering the man.

Ensuring that he would never be forgotten.

And she felt better.

Hopeful.

"You know," Kyra said, hugging her sister tightly, "Ryan really *would* enjoy this."

Chapter 15

After a long, sleepless night filled with too much thinking, Kyra finally came to a decision. She'd spent most of her life hiding from love. Afraid to allow any tenderness into her life for fear of losing control.

Well, she'd been alone. Been tough. And she'd lost control anyway.

It was time to stop pretending that love didn't matter. Time to start going after the life she wanted.

And what she wanted, was Garrett.

She just didn't know if he wanted her. He hadn't called. Hadn't tried to see her since their return to

Red Rock. And let's face it, if he'd wanted to, she just wouldn't have been that hard to find.

A small, insecure voice in the back of her mind whispered that by staying away, he was cutting his losses. Protecting himself by keeping distance between them.

If that were true, though, he was going to have to say so to her face. She wouldn't walk away from what might be because of fear. Not anymore.

Before she could confront Garrett, however, she had to fight her way through the feeding frenzy of news media at the ranch's front gate.

Face down the accusations against her.

It wouldn't be easy.

As a member of the Fortune family, she'd long ago made peace with the fact that they were all considered fair game. They'd been fodder for legitimate magazines and newspapers for years, not to mention the tabloids. She could even remember as a kid seeing one of those grocery store scandal sheets spouting the headline Fortune Family in League with Aliens!

There was simply no hiding from people determined to get a story. So she'd decided last night, during one of her interminable cups of hot cocoa, to face the monsters. To do what she had to do to win back her life. To fix it so that she could go see Garrett again. Make him admit that what they'd shared in that cabin hadn't been a fantasy but the only real thing either of them had felt in years.

Steeling herself, she stepped out of the dollhouse of a guest cottage and onto the stone path that led through a well-tended garden and past a small stand of trees. Gray clouds scudded overhead, intermittently blotting out the sun.

Kyra shivered and wondered if those gray clouds were some sort of omen. Maybe Ryan, telling her to go hide again? At that thought, she laughed shortly. Ryan Fortune had never backed down from a fight in his life.

She'd learned a lot from him over the years. And had even learned quite a bit at his funeral. Her steps sure and steady on the stone path, she thought about the wake and the realizations that had continued to slam into her during those long hours.

Family, she thought firmly. Everything was rooted in family. And the love that bound people together. She'd tried to go through life a solitary creature, with the idea of protecting herself from hurt. But what could possibly hurt more than growing old all alone? Of never knowing what it was to love and be loved in return, or having children, watching them grow and find others to love?

And by the same token, what could be more important than continuing the legacy of love and family that Ryan Fortune had left for them all?

A sudden, sharp wind slapped at her, as if urging

her back into the sanctuary of the guest cottage. But she wouldn't give in to the urge to hide anymore. She'd done enough of that.

It was time to strike back. She tugged the edges of her deep blue sweater together and quickened her steps toward the front of the ranch. The flat heels of her black mules clacked against the stones and sounded like an erratic heartbeat.

Her mouth was dry and her stomach a tangle of raw nerves. She slapped one hand against her abdomen in an effort to ease the bats flying around inside, but it didn't help.

Nothing would, she knew, until she'd faced the ravening hordes waiting for her.

"Oh, boy," she whispered as she rounded a bend in the path and stopped dead. A hundred yards away, at the end of the wide, flower-lined drive, the reporters were still gathered, and the clamor they made reached out to her like a warm welcome into hell.

Oh, she really didn't want to do this. Especially alone. But there was little choice. She was the one they wanted and she couldn't and wouldn't hide behind her family indefinitely.

Lifting her chin, Kyra headed down the middle of the drive. It didn't take long for the mob to notice her. Instantly, cameras swung in her direction and eager reporters clung to the wrought-iron gates and shouted questions at her.

She kept her steps slow and even. She wouldn't

let them know how shaken she was. How nervous. How alone she felt. As she got closer to the crowd, the questions grew louder, more demanding.

"Ms. Fortune, is it true you're a party to an alleged monopoly?"

She winced but kept walking.

"Ms. Fortune, is there really a warrant out for your arrest?"

Jail? she thought with a silent shriek.

Another reporter shouted, "Ms. Fortune, our viewers want to know the real story at Voltage Energy."

"Then you should listen to me."

Kyra stopped just short of the gates. That one, deep, so familiar voice cut through the babble and silenced them all with the ring of authority. Her breath coming short and fast, she twisted her head, sweeping her gaze back and forth across the crowd. She winced when the sun came out and glinted off the lenses of cameras, piercing her eyes. But she couldn't stop looking. Couldn't stop hoping that she hadn't imagined that voice.

As the sea of reporters fell back, allowing a man and a woman to pass, Kyra caught her breath. It *was* Garrett, holding his admin assistant, Carol, firmly by the elbow. He stepped up to the gates and stared at her.

His eyes were impossible to read. But wasn't

it enough that he was here? That he'd come to the ranch to find her? To face the reporters?

Oh God, yes.

Her stomach still churned wildly, but there was a sense of hope fluttering in her chest.

"Who're you?" someone asked.

Before Garrett could answer, another, better prepared reporter shouted, "Mr. Wolff! Do you have an official statement to make?"

Garrett's gaze caught and held Kyra's for what felt like forever, but was probably no more than a few seconds. Then he was turning his back on her to face the crowd gathering around him like piranhas swarming a piece of raw meat.

"As most of you already know, my name is Garrett Wolff," he said in a loud, clear and calm voice. "I'm executive vice president of the expansion division at Voltage."

The crowd rumbled, cameras clicked and video cameras hummed.

"I, and my administrative assistant, Carol Summerhill," he said, indicating the woman at his side with a jerk of his head, "have already given our statements to the police. We're here now so she can clear up a few matters for you people."

Carol? Kyra thought. What could the woman possibly have to say that would help? But Kyra was as intrigued as the reporters, and walked quietly down the drive until she was separated from Garrett only by the strong iron bars of the gate.

A long pause ticked past before Carol started talking. When she did, her voice was hushed and strained, but every word was clear.

"I made it up," she said, trying to pull free of Garrett's grasp. "I invented the story of the monopoly. I lied about Ms. Fortune."

Excitement pulsed and the crowd moved closer, practically salivating. Garrett released the woman and she immediately started pushing her way through the melee, trying to fight her way upstream. As the reporters followed the latest story, Garrett was left alone at the gate.

Slowly, he turned to face Kyra. He grabbed the iron bars and gave them a shake. "You going to let me in?"

"She lied? About all of it?" Kyra's head was still spinning. She'd known Carol was a weirdo, but this was really over the top. Kyra hardly noticed as the reporters fired up their vehicles and took off in a ratty little convoy, following Carol as she drove away at a breakneck pace.

"She did."

"But why?"

His fists tightened around the cold iron. "Doesn't matter. Not anymore," he declared, shaking the bars again as though if he held on tightly enough, he could make them open, could get beyond the last barrier separating him from Kyra. "The point is, the police are convinced."

"But," Kyra said, glancing down the now empty road, "she just got away."

"She won't get far." He tossed a glance behind him, then looked back at Kyra. "I talked Sergeant Donovan into letting me bring her here, to get this out as quickly as possible. But the police are waiting for her at her apartment."

"You mean it's over?" Kyra asked.

"For us," he agreed. "The higher-ups at Voltage might have some explaining to do. Seems they really *were* going to try for a monopoly." He still couldn't believe it, and shook his head at the stupidity of those in charge. "Carol said she made it all up, but as it turns out, it was a lucky guess."

The sun came out from behind another cloud and bathed the two of them in a splash of golden light.

"I don't know what to say," Kyra admitted.

Garrett just stared at her. Her eyes looked tired, as if she'd been as haunted as he these last few days. But there was a glint of steel in those blue-green depths that he admired. That he'd missed seeing.

And if he didn't get his hands on her in the next few minutes, he was going to lose what was left of his mind.

"That's good," he said tightly. "Because I've got a few things to say to *you,* so you can just listen."

"Really?" she asked, folding her arms around her

middle and hanging on. "And why do I want to do that?"

"Because I love you," he said.

She blinked. "Oh."

Not exactly the response he'd been hoping for, but at least she hadn't screamed and run for the hills.

"Are you going to open this damn gate or are you going to make me climb it?"

She grinned, fast and sweet. "You think you could?"

He pinned her with a hungry look. "To get to you? No problem."

"I'd actually like to see that," she said, "but maybe another time." Then she quickly stepped to the far edge of the gate, punched in a code on an electronic keypad, and the iron barrier opened with a slow creak.

Garrett stepped through the moment he could, and wasted no time getting to Kyra. Holding her close, he wrapped his arms around her and held on as if afraid someone would come along and snatch her out of his grasp.

"God, I missed you."

"I missed you, too."

"I love you," he whispered, almost strangling on the raw emotions choking him. Then he pulled back, looked down into her eyes and lost himself there. "I want you to know I've never said that before. Not to anyone."

"But—"

"Not even to my former fiancées. Maybe I knew that they weren't the ones. That it wasn't right. Somehow, on some level, I must have known. But this time I'm sure. And I'm not afraid to say it anymore. I think I always knew there was something between us, Kyra."

"Garrett—"

"Let me finish." He hurried on, not giving her a chance to speak until he'd said everything that had been clawing at him for the last two days. "That night in the cabin…that was the first time I've felt really alive in years. And it's because of you. You're everything I want. Everything I need."

"Oh, Garrett…"

"Not finished."

"Sorry." She smiled again and blinked away tears that slid unheeded down her cheeks.

"I know you don't want to be married," he said, though the taste of the words was bitter. He wanted to marry her. To have a family with her. He wanted the two of them to grow old and crochety together. To have amazing fights and wonderful make up sessions. But if she couldn't or wouldn't marry him, then he'd find a way to deal with it.

"I know you don't want kids, either. And I'll try to accept that. But I want to be with you. I want to live with you. Love you. Even if you never want the rest of it, I want you to want me."

"Garrett—"

"Still talking," he said, and dropped a fast kiss on her mouth in an attempt to silence her. "We'll be good together, Kyra. We'll laugh. We'll love. You won't be sorry."

"I know."

"I—" He broke off, stunned. "What?"

"I said, I know we'll be good together." She reached up to lay one hand against his cheek. "I've missed you so much."

"Thank God," he said, and turned his face into her palm to kiss it.

"And I want to get married," she told him.

"You do?" He looked at her, and saw everything he'd hoped to see there in her face. His heart thundered in his chest and his blood roared triumphantly in his veins.

"I do," she said, nodding, smiling. "And I want kids, too. A lot of 'em. In the last couple of days, I've finally realized just how important family is. How necessary it is."

"Works for me," he said, pulling her close for another rib-crushing hug. Then he took her mouth in a kiss he'd spent days fantasizing about.

She melted into him, her arms wrapping around his neck as she pressed her body to his. Made for each other, he thought absently as he dived into the sensations only she could arouse in him.

And when the kiss ended, he brushed her hair

back from her face and smiled again. "There's one more thing."

"What's left?" she asked, grinning.

"I'm unemployed," he admitted. "I told Voltage what they could do with their job this morning, and then I walked out."

"It just so happens," Kyra said, still feeling the magic of his kiss sizzling through her, "that I have an in at Fortune TX, Ltd. If you're interested, your fiancée could probably put in a good word for you."

"Well, she is a terrific woman."

"I know she's glad you think so," Kyra said, feeling the years of anxiety and worry and fear that she wasn't quite good enough melt away.

With Garrett, she felt whole. She felt complete. And she felt an incredible hope for the future.

"I do love you," she said. "In fact, I was coming to you this morning to tell you so."

"And I love you." He stopped, grinned and said it again. "I love you. Sounds good, doesn't it?"

"It sounds perfect," she exclaimed, and stepped into his arms again. Together, she and Garrett would build a family that Ryan Fortune would be proud of.

Because with family, Kyra thought, all things were possible.

While Kyra and Garrett made their plans for the future, Emmett Jamison walked the path that Ryan Fortune had walked so often in his life.

He barely noticed the ranch land, the outbuildings or the ranch hands working around him. Instead, he stared at a distant image only he could see.

Rage seethed within him and he fought to control it. To focus it. His boots scuffed to a stop on the path as he tipped his head back to gaze at the cloud-filled sky above him. He stared hard enough to try to see beyond the clouds to the heavens where Ryan Fortune was, no doubt, looking down on them all.

And talking to the man he'd admired so much, Emmett made him another promise.

"It's a hard thing for a man to admit about his own brother," he whispered fervently. "But Jason is just no damn good. I'm sorry, Ryan, for all the pain he caused you in a time when you should have been able to claim some peace."

Emmett's heart ached, his soul stung as he said forcefully, "And I promise you, somehow or other, I will see to it personally that Jason Jamison pays."

* * * * *

FAMOUS FAMILIES

YES! Please send me the *Famous Families* collection featuring the Fortunes, the Bravos, the McCabes and the Cavanaughs. This collection will begin with 3 FREE BOOKS and 2 FREE GIFTS in my very first shipment— and more valuable free gifts will follow! My books will arrive in 8 monthly shipments until I have the entire 51-book *Famous Families* collection. I will receive 2-3 free books in each shipment and I will pay just $4.49 U.S./$5.39 CDN for each of the other 4 books in each shipment, plus $2.99 for shipping and handling.* If I decide to keep the entire collection, I'll only have paid for 32 books because 19 books are free. I understand that accepting the 3 free books and gifts places me under no obligation to buy anything. I can always return a shipment and cancel at any time. My free books and gifts are mine to keep no matter what I decide.

268 HCN 9971   468 HCN 9971

Name	(PLEASE PRINT)	
Address		Apt. #
City	State/Prov.	Zip/Postal Code

Signature (if under 18, a parent or guardian must sign)

Mail to the **Reader Service:**

IN U.S.A.: P.O. Box 1867, Buffalo, NY 14240-1867
IN CANADA: P.O. Box 609, Fort Erie, Ontario L2A 5X3

* Terms and prices subject to change without notice. Prices do not include applicable taxes. Sales tax applicable in N.Y. Canadian residents will be charged applicable taxes. This offer is limited to one order per household. All orders subject to approval. Credit or debit balances in a customer's account(s) may be offset by any other outstanding balance owed by or to the customer. Please allow 4 to 6 weeks for delivery. Offer available while quantities last. Offer not available to Quebec residents.

Your Privacy- The Reader Service is committed to protecting your privacy. Our Privacy Policy is available online at www.ReaderService.com or upon request from the Reader Service.
We make a portion of our mailing list available to reputable third parties that offer products we believe may interest you. If you prefer that we not exchange your name with third parties, or if you wish to clarify or modify your communication preferences, please visit us at www.ReaderService.com/consumerchoice or write to us at Reader Service Preference Service, P.O. Box 9062, Buffalo, NY 14269. Include your complete name and address.

FFBPA11